TRIFECTA

TRIFECTA

Ian Wedde

Victoria University Press

VICTORIA UNIVERSITY PRESS
Victoria University of Wellington
PO Box 600 Wellington
vup.victoria.ac.nz

First published 2015

National Library of New Zealand Cataloguing-in-Publication Data

Wedde, Ian.
Trifecta / Ian Wedde.
ISBN 978-0-86473-983-4
I. Title.
NZ821.3—dc 23

This book was written with the support of the Creative New Zealand
Berlin Writers' Residency 2013–14.

Published with the support of a grant from

Printed by Printlink, Wellington

Mick

Every day the same I'm waiting for him at the bottom of my street, rain or shine. Flat tack around the corner pushing that old wooden toy lawnmower towards the corner dairy where Mrs Patel will be singing along to a CD, waving her fingers loaded with rings. The others come after in dribs and drabs, mooing and giggling. It's a highlight in their day. The one they call Push has the edge on them despite the wooden mower. What happens if they get in front of him can be entertaining or ugly depending on your attitude to the mentally feeble.

It's pissing down but I let Push go first as usual. His minder's keeping up okay but it's an effort, the so-called New World Syndrome. She's got the wooden lawnmower to thank for her daily workout. She gives me a wave and a smile stretched to its limit by exertion. Push rams the mower into a blocked storm-drain grille and begins to yell when it gets stuck in the flood. He yells as if someone's tearing his toenails out with pliers—right up there at the top end of what any listener could handle, shrill, ear-splitting, with fragments of word-shapes hurt past recognition. You can tell what he was like as a kid. He still is. But his age comes as a shock when you get close enough to his weepy little red eyes and badly shaved top lip, the few snaggly teeth sticking out under it.

To her credit Push's hefty minder goes in over her

ankles getting the mower past the soggy dam of leaves and paper and back on the footpath. On they gallop around the corner by the tinnie house. There's a hint of aromatic relaxant in the air. Bit early for a smoke. A couple of tuis are trading insults in the Norfolk pine, one of them sounds like a car alarm, the other like a doorbell. They could be courting. Excited dogs are yelping up in the misty Town Belt, they could be having fun. The rain drifts down off the hill with a smell of rotting foliage in it. Behind me the rest of the crew are making good progress, hooting and shrieking. The street's sounding like the Amazonian rainforest as the dawn chorus heralds a brand new day.

Mrs Patel is an exotic creature. First thing in the morning she has a dreamy look as she sings along as if some pomaded Bollywood matinee idol with drowsy eyelids is gliding into the shop instead of Push with his two-dollar coin. Her son, an earnest high-school lad with glasses, hands over the two-dollar lolly mixture with one hand while dealing to the till with the dextrous fingers of the other—a virtuoso performance he's been perfecting ever since he had to stand on a box to see over the counter. I've watched him every ka-ching of the way. He'll be off soon, finished the early morning shift. In the evening he'll be back at the till doing his homework under the counter. I wonder if I'll be around on the day he discovers he's stuck there and begins to scream like Push in the storm-drain.

I get in quickly for my smokes. He knows the brand—his fourteen-year-old moustache flinches off his teeth in a smile but his eyes are on the doorway where the halfway-housers are jostling for pole position. Outside is the elderly, gloomy one who won't go into the dairy so wanders into the road and stops the buses while his minder gets him smokes instead of lollies. It amazes me that they let these people smoke. It also amazes me that someone short on brain function can be sad. Push has already rattled off down the hill with his minder puffing behind. He's on his way around the block homeward bound steering the wooden mower. That must be all the exercise he'll get on any day, poor little bugger.

I don't know what it is about the predictable detail of these morning rites that's fascinating, given how nasty boredom makes me.

'Jesus, you're a nasty bugger, Mick!' That would be my sister Veronica—Vero for short as in truth. She bores me witless. Her conversation is like do-up wallpaper, no sooner chosen than in need of replacement. Whereas Push's morning gallop down the home straight, the huffing and puffing field that follows, and the erotic sound of Mrs Patel's sing-along do not. Bore me.

My even more boring brother Sandy would haul out his tattered lecture notes at this point and bore me with the doctrine of, quoting someone, 'man as an animal suspended in webs of significance he himself has spun'. He means culture but what I see are spurts of endorphic excitement firing up the neurotransmitters all the way around the block and then back to the crooning catatonia of the halfway house where the liberated-from-culture zombies get re-zonked.

I don't know either what it is about pulling the cellophane off a fresh packet of smokes and opening the top on that neat arrangement of filter-tips, but my spirits lift every time I do it. It's the small things, the small things, the little symmetries. The sense of disinterested order. Another one is the blackboard breakfast sign outside the Cambridge. It never changes. One smoke gets me down the hill and across Kent Terrace at the lights by Super Liquor. The universe is an orderly place that keeps the essentials within reach.

My newspaper's available at the Lotto shop by the pub where even the obsequious owner's inquiry about my intention to buy a ticket (or not) is predictable.

'Jackpot's up to five mill?' He's holding my newspaper change back as if I might be amused. Also he's speaking in questions as if that's more friendly. Believe me, he's looking down the once-too-often barrel. One day I'll tell him what I'm capable of doing with that kind of money. But yesterday, today, tomorrow, my change is the price of the day's first coffee.

'Have a nice day?'

I intend to. Now give me the fucking change.

The backpackers who rest up at the Cambridge in preparation for their next Kiwi Adventure bus trip sometimes risk the dining room. A few are moving thoughtfully along the breakfast buffet's chafing dishes. Over at the counter Nancy has that patient expression she gets when she's measuring their all-you-can-eat expectations.

'Mick.'

'Nancy.'

There's that whiff of Listerine PocketMist on her breath, Jameson's under. I find it cheering on a rainy day like this, as I do Nancy's smile which this morning seems false.

Some mornings I can almost hear my brother Sandy's encouraging tone as he lectures his students about social distinction, cultural capital and status anxiety. On the rare occasions we phone he talks to me as if I'd booked office time with him. I like my coffee thin, black and stewed, from the decanter. I like my fried eggs centred on a piece of toast. I like to have my newspaper open on the table to the left of my plate. The best table is the one where the paper gets plenty of light on it. On sunny mornings this is by the window. Today it's in the far corner booth with a wall lamp to one side. I keep my reading glasses in a hard case that makes a good loud noise when it snaps shut. It makes the backpackers jump. Yes, I'm like that. In Sandy's world all this would mean far too much and he'd know far too much about the meaning.

Nancy's insincere smile means she's got something on her mind and that she's going to tell me about it. And it means she already knows my breakfast order. So what? Unlike Sandy I'm not compelled to go deeper. She's known what I have for breakfast ever since she started work here which was after the refurbishment five years ago. Do I miss the smell of cigarettes and lard? And at least a generation of beery farts around the bar stools beyond the dining room? I like Nancy's aroma better. It's homely, apple shampoo or something on top of the breath freshener and the Irish, and I also like it when she sits down beside me for a quick chat. She pats my hand to emphasise what she's saying.

She's read about my house in the paper, page two. The funny square red one.

I ignore that. Her youngest daughter's pregnant again, number three. Nancy reckons the girl's got some kind of hidden attractor that sucks blokes in and chucks them out. They never stick around longer than the first trimester. Sandy would have some kind of cultural explanation for that but Nancy and I know it's evolutionary biology at its purest.

'Hell's teeth, I dunno, Mick. "The condom broke." What was the dope using, Gladwrap? The one before this she said she believed she was in the safe zone, monthly-wise. *Believed.* What does she think she is, a Catholic? This last one was a bike courier.'

'Express delivery.'

'Probably kept his helmet on, he was out of there that fast.'

'You'd think those tight shorts might do the trick.'

'Clearly did. Another cup?'

'Drop the sperm count, I mean. Yes please, Nancy.'

Probably the girl just likes having babies and likes athletes to have them with. I don't say this to Nancy because she knows it already. She probably liked having them herself and with athletes for all I know but I don't say that either.

When she puts my second cup down, Nancy pauses.

'What?' I ask.

She's looking at me, so I take my glasses off.

'Nothing.'

Glasses back on. I read that Real Deal helped bury a Gold Coast hoodoo for veteran trainer Corker Wood when she won the Magic Millions Classic across the Taz on Saturday.

Halfway across the room, Nancy turns and comes back.

'That house of yours,' she says.

Here we go.

I keep the glasses on. Wood's filly pulled down $2 million for that race. Gundy Boy paid $31 in the MM Cup. Win some, lose some.

'Never mind,' says Nancy.

If I'd wanted a housekeeper let alone a careless one like Nancy's daughter with three bastard brats I wouldn't be sitting where I am now. And Nancy wouldn't be stamping away with smoke coming off her. A burly, red-haired bloke in complicated shorts is feeling the heat of Nancy's glare on his neck as he tests the capacity of his breakfast buffet plate. His ears begin to redden like the sky above bushfires in his native land. I'm no more responsible for the spark that just lit Nancy's tinder than I am for the Black Saturday fire that nearly roasted British General four years ago, $10 at Flemington last Saturday, fuck it.

Nor am I responsible for the newspaper's keen interest in my home. The item on page two has Sandy's territorial piss all over it. Vero's too probably, if she could aim straight—the house is on her Heritage Trail.

Let's see, what would I rather live in, my own home, an architectural icon, or a heritage site? Nancy's expression on her fourth return this morning adds another option: a house with four empty bedrooms and one selfish prick. She plonks my plate of eggs and toast on the table.

'Don't let them get cold.'

'Thanks, Nancy.' I've no idea what she means by that. None whatsoever. I have less trouble getting the hang of the newspaper article. Not the meaning of the words on the page, their easy-to-grasp account of one of New Zealand's modernist masterpieces, its 'austere elegance unmatched in post-World War Two domestic architecture'. Rather, the meaning of why the account is there on page two at all. Together with the all-too-familiar image of the coloured squares and rectangles attributed to the influence of Farkas Molnár. *In 'the literature'.* Or rather, to keep it simple, the meaning of why I'm still there in the 'neglected' masterpiece. Why, why, why am I still there? Why is the place falling to bits? Where's the furniture gone? All those fucking knock-offs of Marcel Breuer and other cultural icons who wouldn't know a comfortable chair in which to jerk off if they saw it by the light of their spindly anglepoise lamps. Questions, questions, questions flooding the mind of the curious young person today. *This* is what the words mean—Sandy might as well have drawn a map for culture vultures and stuck an interpretive text on my front door. Chucked up a website. Or got a cultural petition circulating among professional architectural cognoscenti who have no business knowing let alone caring where or how I live. In the house that's as much mine as theirs. My brother's and sister's, I mean. More, if you take into account the fact that I actually live in the fucking thing.

The fork that lifts egg to my mouth is trembling and a blob of yolk falls on the item about Maestro's bruised heel. He's not being entered for the Trentham Telegraph. His trainer Jim Tell reports, 'I took him to a lovely fresh grass paddock on our new Cambridge property and he walked to one side and introduced himself to the horses in the adjoining paddock then introduced himself to the horses on the other side then mooched to the middle of the paddock and started grazing. He announced that he was in town and left it at that.' Now that's a beautiful piece of writing, accurate, vivid, evocative, if a little anthropomorphic, no hidden meanings just plenty to think about, and it leaves Maestro where he may safely graze in his home paddock.

'Where are you calling from?' I can tell from the overconfident timbre of my brother's voice that he's shitting himself. Perhaps he thinks I'm really in Phuket throwing trust funds at whores.

No, he thinks I've read the paper.

'Payphone at the Courtenay Place TAB.' It's the truth but Sandy's silence says he thinks I'm winding him up.

'What's the matter, Mick?'

'And a very good morning to you too, Sandy. Professional intellectual track not too heavy for you today?' I can hear the air whistling in and out of Sandy's nostrils. There's that funny glottal click as he swallows. 'Still the odds-on favourite, Sandy? With the young crowd?'

'What do you want, Mick.' He says this as though it isn't a question.

You can't say I didn't try. 'I was hoping you could help me with a conceptual matter, Sandy. If you've got a moment.' Nostrils, glottal clicks, and other sounds that suggest Sandy's trying to get dressed with a cellphone between shoulder and ear. 'Tell me if this isn't convenient, Sandy.'

'I'm at the gym.'

'Is that convenient or inconvenient?'

'Just tell me what you want.'

'See, here's the thing.' There are certain expressions Sandy refers to as 'memes'—he's too much of a snob to pretend he doesn't despise them.

'The *thing*.'

'Yes, Sandy, the thing. See, there's this horse I think's going to hit his straps any day now, he's called Maestro, beautiful young chestnut thoroughbred, he's got a sore foot at the moment so he's been pastured, you know, allowed to stay at home for a bit, at home, Sandy, he's a happy animal, bit anthropocene of me, I know, to say that, given that he's been bred to entertain me and with any luck restore my fortunes, but leaving that aside, do you have any thoughts at all about the *cultural* dimension of an animal feeling happy and at home, Sandy? I've pretty much got the evolutionary aspect sussed, not to mention the endorphic happiness produced by a good feed of grass, but I need help with the wider social and cultural aspects, your field I believe. What's your advice? Think the happy horse is worth a punt?'

'Shut the fuck up, Mick, and stop wasting my time.'

'No, Sandy, you stop wasting some poor young star-struck arts page reporter's time getting my place plastered all over the paper, you miserable prick.'

'*Our* place.'

I hang up. I for one have no doubt that Jim Tell is doing the right thing by Maestro. That horse will be happy and ready to hit his straps when the time is right. A runner's high will be his reward when the neurotransmitters kick in over the last furlong, and my payoff something not dissimilar.

I'd been in such a hurry to get from my breakfast to the phone at the TAB I'd missed out on my after-breakfast smoke, so I step from the neon glare into the murky rain outside and light up. The usual deadshits are hanging about. The only reason I can come up with is that they hope to catch the eye of someone who's just struck it lucky or exercised their finely tuned powers of odds analysis, whichever is most likely at the time. Alternatively the smelly, wheedling folk are there because this is a magnetic field of bad luck into whose orbit those convinced they are steered by rational thought are drawn. I give the young dude in the filthy sleeveless puffer jacket a cigarette. The old ones can get fucked, they've had all the chances they're going to get. It's not conversation I want but my Sandy-agitated ticker is still thumping away so I'm willing to be asked a friendly question.

'Can you hear them? They're under the ground. There's thousands of them. The tiny burning Bibles.' The dude's cheeks disappear into his face as he draws on the smoke I've given him. His eyes have the endearing, personable look of someone whose moral dynamo is innocently grit-free. The answer to his question is no, I can't hear the thousands of tiny burning Bibles under the ground. But he can, apparently.

'Can you?' I ask.

He sweeps his arm around the damp vista of Courtenay Place—the glistening footpath, the bus shelters with their huddled masses in outdoorsy gear, the pristine new toilets whose chic neo-modernist aesthetic reminds me of my newly famous home, the massive Transformer-like monument to New Zealand's film industry down the far end that Sandy 'loathes' and Vero has on her 'must-see' cultural hot-spots schedule, the welcoming lights of the mini-mart, the strip joint a few doors up from which comes a weary morning-after subwoofer bass thud. I'm guessing his gesture means yes, they're all over the place, all under the place.

And considered from another perspective I'm tempted to say yes, I can too, now that you mention it. I can hear the tiny burning Bibles under there. After all, the dude wasn't asking if there could be thousands of tiny burning Bibles under the ground, only if I could hear them (if they were there). And if by thousands of tiny burning Bibles I'm to understand doubt, that accelerant to the incineration of rational belief, then yes. Yes, I can hear that sound—indeed I'm standing outside the very temple of doubt as we speak. And Nancy's words come back to mind: '*Believed.* What does she think she is, a Catholic?'

My path is lit by them, the burning Bibles.

'Thanks, dude,' I say, and give him the whole packet. He's lucky but he's just made me luckier.

Inside, I put five grand on a Final Touch, Xanadu and Burgundy trifecta for the Trentham Telegraph this afternoon. The sound of thousands of tiny burning Bibles. Maestro grazing the sweet grass of his home paddock, out of the running, no chance. It's got nothing to do with belief. Burn it. Cauterise it. Burn the Bibles. That peptide rush of certainty. When in doubt, don't.

Wonton Phil's looking at me funny. He stops yabbering into the cellphone mike hanging around his neck. 'What you got, Micky?' The one lank strand of hair he has left is plastered athwart his pale, perspiring skull. It's like a signpost pointing ninety degrees away from where he's looking—he should pay more attention to it.

'Benefit of the doubt,' I say.

Wonton doesn't get it. Trentham, 5.45 p.m. start—I'll be celebrating at The Honeysuckle by teatime.

Time to stretch the legs.

Habit, routine, groove, call it what you like, my daily walk around Oriental Bay is both always the same and always different. In fact what's the same about it is that it's always different. That's because Oriental Bay never realigns itself overnight so the city's on my right going north. No, the fountain's impersonation of a whale spouting always has the city's glass towers flashing beyond it to the west. The bulk of Mount Victoria has always been at my right shoulder as I set off heading north, and my father was always, always keeping stride at my left shoulder—Marty preferred that side, the one nearest the water. If I ever tried to change places with him he'd outmanoeuvre me, feinting in front of me then ducking behind and crossing sides between the sea wall and a park bench so I couldn't defend against his move without bashing my knees. Then he'd speed up and come out beyond the bench, on my left (or on my right coming back again, heading south).

'Oh no you don't!'

Time to strrretch the legs.

Marty still spoke such phrases with self-satisfied precision, as if pleased with himself for having learned to master the vernacular.

Once, in the house he designed or, as some whispered, copied from Farkas Molnár—the one that's shoving its blocky coloured squares and rectangles into my head as I *strrretch my legs* at speed around Oriental Bay—he cheerfully invited Sandy to climb up on top of the grand piano. Veronica and I were watching. It was 'family activities time' in the big downstairs living room. We were taking turns doing 'crazy things'. Sandy stood up on top of the piano with a smile of terror and triumph on his face, because this was completely forbidden, to climb on the piano, you couldn't even open it and muck around with the keys, you had to practise *when it is your turn.* But there Sandy stood, torn between triumph at our expense and terror at the transgression he'd been commandeered into. And below him stood Marty, stretching out his long thin arms.

'Now, Sandy, chump to Daddy!'

This was an exciting game.

Sandy jumped while looking at Veronica and me with that weird grin on his face, and our father, whom his friends called Marty, whose proper name was Martin, who was called Marty most of the time, stepped aside and let Sandy crash to the floor.

'Never trrrust anybody!'

He said this in the gloating tone that was the mark of his confident ability to speak in the ordinary vernacular. Then everybody, including Vero and me, but not Marty, began to scream. Our mother was screaming too though she never seemed to be there until the moment of crisis. Marty stood with his long, thin, black-hairy shanks wide apart as if still braced to catch the child he'd told to jump, and ignored our mother's screams, even though she was calling him a fucking bastard. Or rather he just stared the screams down. She was holding Sandy who wasn't really hurt but who was clinging to her with his gulping face in her neck and his legs refusing to unbend, as if the floor was covered in poisonous snakes or was a bottomless pond or, at that moment, had become his father's arms. Which he'd folded while the family stopped screaming, because Marty had begun to laugh. Should we join in? Our mother didn't think so—she carried Sandy, clinging to her front like a marsupial, from the room.

'Well, then,' said our father, still chuckling, '*that didn't go down very well.*'

Yes, what's the same about stretching my legs around Oriental Bay is the geography where I'm doing it and the fact that I am as usual stretching them, and what's not the same is what doing this makes me think about, which is different most days. It's even more different than usual today because I haven't thought about my father and the famous piano-chumping incident for years, and haven't had ringing dully in my ears the fatuous tone of Marty's joke, '*That didn't go down very well.*'

Did I know it was a joke at the time when I was perhaps only five, a year younger than Sandy and one older than Vero? I must have. I couldn't have. I'm making it up. The tinny sound of Marty's joke goes round and round in my head as I reach Point Jerningham, rotate the city to my right and head back along the Parade. The joke sounds too much like one of mine. But then maybe that's why I remember it. I am my father's son. There's some of Martin Klepka in me.

The sun is coming out, little kids are riding little bikes through the puddles, the usual self-absorbed, irritated-looking runners are dodging past them. Everything is the same. But I can't dislodge from my mind the image of Marty's impervious smile, his dark-hairy shanks, and my retreating mother's back with Sandy's legs wrapped around her bottom, trying not to touch the floor, or not to be not caught again, and back to my father's laughter where he stood with folded arms and skinny legs wide apart, staring at Vero and me until we joined in, until he had us both 'in fits'. Then he walked out of the room. This marked the end of 'family activities time'.

I stop outside Freyberg Pool. Sandy used to come

here—he was pedantic about fitness even before his voice broke. A smell of health emanates from the place, nuanced by chlorine. People flushed post-swim are ordering freshly squeezed juices and vegetables from the kiosk at the front. I saw Sandy once pretending not to see Marty and me strrretching our legs. He was sucking on a straw. And there they are again, Sandy's abject legs clinging to the still youthful shape of my mother's backside as she carts him out of range of his father's scornful laughter. Marty's gaze has settled on me, not on Veronica, who already bores him.

I was Marty's favourite. He was sarcastic to Sandy and bored by Vero. But he liked playing *strrretching the legs* harbour-side tag with me. On the occasion of Sandy's crash from the grand piano Marty's grin rewarded me by transforming both his and my satisfaction into open-mouthed laughter. How we laughed. Of course I didn't understand why at the time but I do now—clenching my resolve around the page two newspaper feature on the house I call home. My pasture.

It's mine. It's mine and Marty's. Who gives a shit if it's a Farkas Molnár knockoff. Along with all Martin Klepka's knockoff Marcel Breuer chairs that still adorn the *culturally distinct* living quarters of the capital city's mandarin class.

'Some things just don't go out of fashion, especially in the provinces,' Marty confided to his favourite son when I was almost old enough to appreciate the joke. Just don't expect me to treat the old fraud's products with the same reverence as the clients who made him rich.

One last thing about that moment at the grand piano when I first saw where my father's favour lay. It was the pattern of my mother's dress where bawling Sandy's heels gripped her bum. Because it was summer she was wearing a light cotton dress. It had a symmetrical pattern on it of simple woodblock ziggurats in rather bleached-out teal. This too probably came around the world with Martin Klepka after the Bauhaus Berlin was closed down by stormtroopers in 1933. Marty's disdained child Sandy was pressing his father's successful ripoff textile against his mother's pelvic architecture, which was minimal as you'd expect in the wife of a high modernist, while staring with an expression of appalled hatred at his younger brother Mick's complicit laughter and his father's derision.

Yes I feel sorry for Sandy. I'm human. But the memory that's made today's leg-stretch different from others has made me feel lucky. It's given me an ego stiffy. I'm liking it.

'Chump to Daddy!'

The old prick wouldn't have caught me either but we'd have understood each other, perhaps. Whereas bawling Sandy didn't and Vero couldn't. Never did and never could, respectively. *How the cookie crumbles*, as our father might have said, with that hint of pedantic smugness.

Never trrrust anybody!

Our father almost never talked about his past. He told me that he had no brothers or sisters, I should count myself lucky. To have a couple. Even if they're not, you know. We were up on scaffolding, repainting the south wall of the house. Marty had splashes of red paint on his face. At first I thought he meant his brothers and sisters had been killed in the war but that's not what he said. About a year later he told me his mother and father had given him money to get out of Germany. He was twenty-seven and went to Spain. It was summer again and we were up on the flat roof this time, laying down new bitumen. I'd asked him how he got here but his answer seemed to be about why his mother and father hadn't.

A couple of years later when he was giving me a driving lesson he told me about being incarcerated as a 'hostile alien' on Somes Island 'with a bunch of Nazis'. The joke was that being Jewish made him a hostile alien among the Nazis of Somes Island, but the real meaning of the joke was 'Never trrrust anybody'. He turned mistrust into an operational virtue. He was serious about it which was probably why he played it for laughs. Once when a couple of nicely suited Mormon missionaries were spotted approaching the house he opened the door wearing nothing but a World War One German helmet with a spike on top and with a hard-on below. The latter was justly famous.

'They won't be back!'

He never spoke of the German Ashkenazim and the family's Polish connection. We heard bits and pieces about these from our mother who was neither German nor Jewish, nor Polish for that matter. But she wouldn't talk about it if Marty was around because it wasn't worth the anger. She told us he left his family behind after the Berlin Bauhaus was raided in 1933. All he ever said about the place was that it was 'an empty telephone factory'. I don't know what he meant—not, anyway, that it was an empty telephone factory, even if it was. He enjoyed talking in riddles, they were like taunts. Later on we all knew about the designs he took with him from 'the empty telephone factory', because of what he was doing, churning out the stuff that made Sandy purse his connoisseur lips and Vero wet herself.

It's always seemed to me that the knockoff Breuer chairs,

the insolently inclined lamps, the simple geometrical fabric patterns, the landscaped gardens and wooden decks opening from glass walls were piled up by Martin Klepka's furious energy into a kind of archly tasteful barricade between himself and whatever might have happened to his mother and father in 1938, when the Polish Jews were deported from Germany and we all know what happened after that. But then I don't know that and my father was never going to tell me. It was forbidden to talk about it, whatever in fact 'it' was. No that's not true, it was never talked about regardless, because Marty's way of staring at you across the table was completely terrifying. When we were kids we used to call it 'the look'.

'It's always seemed to me' isn't true either. The 'always' begins when I was old enough to stop being scared of 'the look' and began to see that Marty wanted me to be the one who'd occupy the future he was knocking himself out to shore up. The future he couldn't have himself because no matter how hard he tried he was always teetering on the edge of a pit or had just overshot the brink and was pedalling furiously at the air like one of those cartoon characters before they drop.

But if Sandy and Vero ever ask me nicely why I've got rid of so much of the stuff in that house they think is also theirs, then I might tell them that it wasn't for the *gelt*—one word from Marty's past that he uttered, albeit with a sardonic spit at the end, although the gelt came in handy. It was because the money I made didn't get in the way of the terrible ghosts that Marty's barricade of high-value manufactured goods was trying to keep out. They could come in as often as they liked as far as I was concerned, the ghosts. They could hoo-hoo around the empty rooms looking for their absconded son, because their son had long ago sunk with all his rage and guilt into the old swamp of the earth where everything turns into shit first and nothing at all next.

Sports Bar coming into view. I love the intelligence of the body. My throat starting to swallow without me having to think 'thirst'.

And the other ghost, Agnes? That was her Scottish grandmother's name. She liked telling us about all that. Often she'd begin a story but then stop. Sometimes she'd start a story halfway through. It was as though the stories were on repeat spools in her mind and she cut in and out of them. Her father was Italian, he used to fish out of Island Bay. He drowned somewhere over in the Karori Rip when she was a baby. He was probably drunk, said Agnes, as if to innoculate us against his condition, though she never knew him. That's where Veronica's name comes from, the Italian. Sandy's really Alistair, that's the Scottish connection. And Mick? That would be Michael wouldn't it, the 'Who is like God?' guy, the only trace left by Marty who remained unsheeted from any family narrative as far as I can tell, fine by me. But there it is.

It does no harm to suggest that my mother's red hair was Celtic but that the crazy bouncing tangle of it, which her hands were always tucking and patting into submission, was from Venice. She promised she'd take us all there. One day. Sandy knows better than to tell me he got there all by himself, and Vero once started to skite to me about her Italian trip with her daughter, but stopped.

Sometimes what my mother's hands were tucking back

into place wasn't her hair but her thoughts. I knew that was what she was doing when she then sat very still and her eyes were not-quite-focused on something between her and the world. Her eyes were shiny and very nearly black but when she was doing that looking-at-nowhere thing they seemed to film over and her eyelids drooped.

All this shit coming back. If I could get my hands around Sandy's scrawny neck I'd choke the tongue out of his head.

The School is halfway down a pre-lunch jug when I come into the Sports Bar. The first thing I see is a copy of today's newspaper on the table. It's not open to the page with the weird red house on it but I know that it will have been. The three of them put their glasses down—what were they toasting?—and look at me.

There's no way I'm going to tell them the story about Sandy jumping off the grand piano, though this is the one that's jostling for track advantage with the memory of my mother Agnes's fingers busy in the thicket of her hair, tucking thoughts back in there.

'Where have you been-been-een?'

Of course the question's a joke. Ratchet knows I've been stretching my legs. But then I am late today. He sees my eyes lift to the TV where the TAB odds are clicking over, and he's not fooled when I look away as if I'm not interested.

'I've been exercising my mind,' I say.

Even that first abstemious swallow of beer pulls the hair-trigger that waits between throat and gut. The shot propels me to the bar where I get another jug and five nips of the Irish that Nancy prefers.

'Jesus Christ-Christ-ist,' says Ratchet. 'What are we marking the passing of today-day-ay?' No one comments on him rearranging the coasters and the nip glasses until he achieves a satisfactory symmetry. Then he blinks three times and downs his nip. Three more blinks. You have to wait until he's run the sequence otherwise he has to start all over again. The collar and sleeves of his jacket are closed tight, his pants are tucked into his socks, his hair is plastered flat with goo, and the remarkable intelligence in there bounces off the walls. 'Another big win-win-in,' he says, flattening the question into a taunt.

I ignore it.

There's also Frank, the only one of us who goes back to work after lunch, and Geordie, who's watching the thin end of an inheritance approach at a steady speed. Frank dresses in an old but good quality suit and is never without a tie closing the border where his silverback body hair meets his shave line. Geordie wears shorts in all weather. He used to run with Scottish Harriers and his skinny legs are all veins and gristle but his knees gave out. Sometimes, that's usually, Nancy joins us from the dining room for a quick Irish.

Here she comes now. Clearly there's something magnetic in the atmosphere.

'How are we, boys?' She accepts the whiskey I nudge towards her and keeps her eyes on me.

'Mick was late,' says Frank. 'We think he's probably hiding something. Meanwhile CPI's up, we were discussing the opportunity costs of our respective dwellings. Or, in my case, my wife's dwelling.'

'How is Fay?' says Nancy, still looking at me. Her top

lip dabs a smidgen of Irish and she holds the vapour of it in her mouth with her lips pursed.

'She's in Bali,' says Geordie. 'Frank was just telling us. There's this organic resort on top of a mountain, with monkeys.'

'They add value, you, ou.'

'The monkeys?' says Nancy. 'Now that's novel. Round here it's the double glazing. So I hear.'

I open the paper, very slowly for dramatic effect, to page two.

'With an ape on the inside,' adds Nancy for good measure.

I take a sip myself. I can feel that endorphic pulse between crop and gut starting to find the beat.

My role at the School is to tell stories. Geordie's is honesty, Frank's is cynicism, and Ratchet's the savant. Nancy's there from time to time to tell us we're all full of shit.

'Let me tell you about the man who built this fucking house.'

Because I'm not going to tell them about the piano, nor about my mother's hair, I tell them about the time my father, Martin Klepka, the well-known interior and landscape designer and sometime architect, took his clothes off and jumped into the sea at Point Jerningham at the turn-around point in our leg-stretch, saying he'd race me back to the band rotunda, me on land, him swimming. Off he went, those wiry arms smashing furiously into the water ahead of him, a churning wake flying up behind him, but with little enough forward movement. I loitered about on the footpath to keep an eye on him but also to give him the chance to beat me.

I wasn't a kid anymore, I'd have been sixteen going on seventeen. I was old enough to know there was something wrong about my father's crazy energy and old enough to match it with what was happening to me, which was sex. The jaw-churning way my father ate, how he reached for more food to put on his plate, the greedy way he leaned into conversations and consumed them, the high colour that lit up his face, his protruding eyeballs, not to mention the mad zest with which he mowed the rectangular lawn at the back of the house, getting the nap into straight light and dark tracks and then sitting with his legs spread drinking a beer with his stringy bag of bollocks hanging out the leg of his shorts—he might as well have been fucking all the time. He didn't embarrass me because I was his favourite and I didn't care what he did. But there was no way I was going to bring a girlfriend home. I saw him trying it on once with one of Sandy's in the back of a minibus going out to a big barbecue wedding in a Wairarapa vineyard. I saw the look on Sandy's face—the ridges across his forehead made him look as if he was clenching his brain.

'So who won?' asks Nancy, thinking she knows the answer.

'Hard to tell,' I say, sidestepping the image of Sandy's anguish. 'He had a heart attack. Mine'll be the fishburger thanks, Nancy, go easy on the tartare. And I'm still in the house.'

There's an ahem kind of silence while Ratchet corrects the coasters and Nancy heads for the kitchen with umbrage stiffening her shoulders.

'Sorry to hear that,' says Frank, taking a pull on his beer. It disappears down his throat into the jungle below and he looks at me with an expression that says he's not.

'Oh, he didn't have it then.' I enjoy the dishonest moment. 'The heart attack, though we had to fish him out.'

'"The Red Cube" cube, ube,' yells Ratchet suddenly. He's quoting the newspaper article, disrespectfully, given that a moment's silence for my father would be appropriate. But he gets agitated when the world and his line of inquiry are out of phase.

'He packed it in about a year later. Only sixty. Then was the time to check the odds-on winners. In the Red Cube stakes, you might say.' I want to keep this light but I'm feeling some pressure, not as much as Ratchet but even so. The Red Cube aka Der rote Würfel. Farkas Molnár project for a single family house, 1922. It had yellow and blue bits as well though this aspect of the concept didn't get as far as Mount Victoria, Wellington, New Zealand. I already know that Farkas barely rates a mention in the article my brother ventriloquised through the compliant *DomPost* arts reporter, because the dishonest, revisionist piece of shit spoiled my breakfast earlier.

Funny thing about history. Marty never minded admitting most of his ideas came from 'the empty telephone exchange', though not in Molnár's case because he was never there. But big brother Sandy feels a need to transform my father's provenance indifference into sentences in which the word 'original' is repeated with guilty frequency, as if writing it often enough is all that's needed to establish the Martin Klepka brand and with it the Martin Klepka fucking brand-value and with that the social distinction and cultural capital of those who bought into Marty's shtick. And with that the resale value of the highly original Red Cube, not referred to in the article as Der rote Würfel because as my brother the distinguished cultural historian knows very well that would light a quick fuse all the way back to 'the empty telephone exchange', which wasn't empty at all. Not at least until it was emptied that day in 1933 when a bunch of people were rounded up but not Sandy's highly original father Martin Klepka.

'Der rote Würfel,' I say, hearing it come out aggressively. I see Ratchet's brain come within a hair's-breadth of making him lose it and start shouting 'Cunt!' or something. But he hangs in there and repositions his glass on the coaster. I see Frank put two and two together but not get a figure he can make sense of.

Maybe I should have flagged lunch today.

Geordie puts his finger on the picture of my red house on page two of the paper. It already has the tell-tale ring of a wet glass on it. I look at the bony finger and then at him until he says what he's thinking.

'They want you out.'

They?

I fill their glasses. Pretty steady hand considering. 'Listen,' I say. 'Here we are, quality minds meeting for lunch and conversation, and you're behaving like a pack of hyenas circling something dead.'

'But is it true?' says Geordie. 'Just tell us, and we'll talk about something else.'

'But what?' says Frank. 'Can you think of anything? My mind's gone blank.' It hasn't of course. It's putting the red house on page two into a matrix of location, Government Valuation, Consumer Price Index and buyer profile. 'And what's a verfel in plain English?'

'Würfel-el-el,' says Ratchet in what sounds like a correcting voice, but he's only chasing the word into his brain.

Frank is looking peevishly at the tube of Ratchet's mouth shaping the foreign word. He's deciding to wind him up. The atmosphere at our table has soured.

I feel close to Ratchet. We've known each other a very long time. At high school he was mainstreamed and tormented. His torment-name was Rat Shit but the protective rage of his crew turned that around. Now it describes accurately what makes him special. His neurotransmitters rattle straight to overdrive. I know what that feels like, for a different reason. And most of what I know about brains comes from Ratchet's.

What Ratchet mostly does is read. I've watched him in the public library, a place we both like though for different purposes. He sits at a table with three or four books to his right and one open in front of him. The finished ones end up to his left. I don't know what kind of hell it is that makes him need exact calibrations of distance between himself and the left and right books, but in between them is a heaven of equilibrium. Ratchet positions a book in line with the direction of his gaze and then begins to turn the pages with his left hand while his right hand keeps the book steady. This is because he just turns the pages one after another. If you sit opposite him and watch his eyes, you see that they shift from left to right taking in whole pages without traversing the lines. Ratchet can get agitated if the book shifts while he's scanning but mostly he keeps it together. Every so often he'll say some words, from the page in front of him you'd think, in a funny robotic voice.

I hear the robot voice today in the Cambridge Sports Bar when Ratchet suddenly shouts, 'Der rote Würfel-el-el!' Of course it's in that impossible brain. He just needed a few seconds to track it down. Then some kind of synapse link flared up like a match struck in a dark room or in an empty telephone exchange for that matter and he had it or had something, what exactly who knows. Ratchet mostly reads maths and physics hence his obsession with supersymmetry. It would be a short path from there to the symmetrical arrangement of cubes by the likes of Farkas Molnár. If their concepts are anything to go by most of Farkas's modernist cronies weren't many clicks away from Ratchet in the obsessive stakes.

'Christ,' says Frank, looking at Rachet with exaggerated pity. 'Not you too.'

Ratchet's staring at me and blinking in sets of three. He's found a short piece of detached string, not the knotted-together answer to everything.

'Würfill, fill, ill,' he says in his normal voice. The clue's a dead-ender.

'We hear you,' says Geordie.

Then there's a silence. We hear that too. I close the newspaper. Geordie opens it again and taps the house. Ratchet positions our glasses on the corners of the page. Up on the TV monitor the drone of a race commentary accelerates, crescendos and diminuendos. Nothing of consequence, not yet but *later*, and then the question of who's a winner and who isn't will be front and centre.

Just to shut the fuckers up.

'When my father died everything went to my mother.

She didn't want the business and sold it. That left the house and money in a trust. When she died her kids all had the right to stay in it but the last one out had to sell up and divvy the proceeds. Has to.' I raise my glass. 'Still half full.'

'One third-ird-ird,' says Ratchet, always on to it.

I'm going to have my work cut out getting back on side with Nancy. She delivers our plates of lunch and leaves again without banter. The School eats its food glumly, eschewing the usual conversational cut and thrust. We make the small talk we have a cast-iron rule against. It's the house on page two that's responsible for this dullness.

'The last time I remember a spring this wet was in . . .' Frank can't remember when it was this wet so he fills his mouth and chews ponderously, as if ruminating a great conceptual cud.

'Two thousand and eleven-ven-en,' says Ratchet, arranging his fries.

'And it's playing havoc with the house market again.' If this is Frank trying to open a line of conversation, I'm going to have business elsewhere.

'Would that be supply-side or demand-side, Frank?' Geordies's eyes duck out from under his eyebrows for just long enough to see me glance at the TV monitor.

'Nancy's daughter's up the duff again, it was a bloke on a bike,' I say, and unless anyone else can match that it's the conversation stopper. But then, just for good measure and because the mention of bad weather makes me think of him, I add, 'Doesn't stop that retard I told you about, the one with the toy mower.'

'What doesn't?' Frank hates losing command of the narrative.

'The rain, Frank,' I say. 'The unusually wet spring. Nor does the poor little bugger much concern himself with real estate.'

Ratchet has his fries in groups of three and is concentrating on polishing them off in an orderly manner.

In the distance (but not too far away) I can glimpse the lights of my triumph. They resemble the warm interior lighting tones of The Honeysuckle, the warm skin tones of Native Bush, and the warm sounds of words like shabu-shabu, yaha, lovey dovey and meow meow. Now that's what I call wet weather.

But first things first.

Frank wipes his mouth and throws the napkin on the table. His work's conveyancing and he gives me a long look before deciding to leave it at that.

'"A fool sees not the same tree that a wise man sees", William Blake. Good afternoon, gentlemen.'

'Yep-yep-yep,' says Ratchet. I've no idea what he has to get away to—the library probably. He'll be looking up the Würfill-fill-ill. He and Frank head for the door. Geordie gets up too but goes to the bar for another jug.

'Come off it, Mick,' he says, topping us up. 'Stop being a spoiled brat. What's eating you? You're twitchier than a . . .'

That's when I see the TV monitor above us run the field and the current odds for the Trentham 5.45. I'm giving it my full attention. Geordie's knuckley hand lands on my arm a bit heavily.

'Sell the fucking thing,' he says. 'Move on.'

Move on.

Final Touch, Xanadu and Burgundy are still lit by that secret glow, the tiny burning Bibles, my prophet's cheeks collapsing on the intake of the oracular smoke, a hiss of tyres on wet asphalt as some things stay put and others move on, and the trigger in my chest fires again as I pour the whole glass down and look Geordie in the eye.

'Christ, Micky, you're not. Tell me you're not doing another cross-green putt.'

I forgive Geordie his mixed sporting metaphor and I forgive him his impertinent solicitude. He plays golf for small change and keeps fit. But I'm not going to give him the satisfaction of saying I'm not wrong this time. Nor inviting him to stay in the pub drinking on me until they run the Trentham Telegraph at 5.45 just so I can say, *See?*—and fall down drunk with righteousness. My afternoon nap is calling but there's something I want to say to Geordie first.

'Let me tell you about the man who built that house,' I begin again.

Geordie looks at me patiently. His eyes are only a bit watery with beer. He's in great shape even though he looks like a strip of biltong. Of all the members of the School I know he's the one who can understand the difference between what happens when you excite the brain by running and when you bewilder it with so-called rational thought and all those appurtenances that rational thought utters such as Marcel Breuer fucking chairs—just to settle on the example that comes quickest to mind. He and I both understand that anything worth knowing comes from old places in the brain that we whip into obsession and that reality is nothing of the sort.

'Steady on, Micky,' says Geordie, though I haven't said anything yet.

'Okay, forget it,' I say. 'Tell me something interesting.'

He looks at me for a wee while. He knows where I'm headed. But he doesn't know about the tidal pull of whatever dream I might be having when I finally get back to the house for my afternoon nap.

Geordie opens his mouth.

'No, hang on,' I say. It's true I'm grinding my teeth and want to punch someone but there's only the wiry little bloke across the table from me and I like him. 'Let me tell you something about the man who built that house.'

Geordie shakes his head slowly from side to side. He's leaving his glass alone but I down mine and pour another.

'The man who built that house liked what he called his afternoon nap. Us kids knew about it on weekends. When we were old enough we understood that it meant fucking. Our mother of course but apparently not always. In our house. There was a fair bit of that sort of thing went on in those days.'

'Not where I come from,' says Geordie. 'He'd have had the back of a frying pan across his head. What, didn't your mother mind?'

'She didn't leave him. Didn't belt him with kitchenware either.' Of course that doesn't answer the question. Nor does it answer the question Geordie's decided not to ask after all.

'"Why, all at once, this renewed interest in your father?"' I mimic Geordie's Scouse accent.

His head goes on one side, like a wee bright-eyed parrot. 'You tell me.'

The bar's filling up with the punter crowd, newspapers are folded open to the racing pages, there are betting slips and copies of *Best Bets* getting wet on the tables and a steady procession of coughing and hacking smokers is going out the door and back in again. What are the triggers that set us off on trajectories that, most days, we have little enough trouble talking ourselves out of? I don't even like how this goes down yet here I am plugged into the mainframe.

'Okay, let me guess,' says Geordie patiently. 'It's that newspaper article, no?'

'It pisses me off.'

'And that's all it takes for you to chuck, let me guess, quite a lot of money down the drain? You're a stupid fucker, Mick. What is this, revenge? Let it go, man.'

Revenge.

'No,' I say. Being cared about is one thing, being patronised another. 'It's about opening up limitless possibilities of action. Intelligence without thought.'

'Fuck's sake,' says the little squirt opposite me. His watery eyes have slitted up.

I put my glass down carefully and walk out into the hissing of tyres on wet asphalt, a baggy grey gaberdine sky, that gritty wind from the north lifting plastic bags into the air. What a dreary shithole this is. I know what I need and I also know that I'm going to have to wait a bit longer for it. The little green man turns red at the lights and I cross at the half-trot just as the traffic gets moving. Horn honks and at least one angry 'you stupid what the fuck'.

One little blue Zopiclone will give me three hours' sound sleep. They say you don't dream but that's bullshit. I have time to spot a good lungful of smoke too before I'm standing in front of the bathroom mirror looking at the skinny, hairy guy with his big purple knob in his hand. His face clenches in a grimace that could be from pain or disappointment, his come surges sluggishly into the handbasin, and when I turn away and head for the bedroom there's a strange event like a toothache in my left temple and an upward surge of nausea in my chest.

I like this room because it faces the back of the house and the bare space where the lawn used to be. The concrete that's there now was screed off to a slick surface that shines after rain, as today, and drags in warmth when it's sunny as will be the case again sooner or later, and the only maintenance required now that the grass has gone is an occasional hose-down which I like to do with no shoes on, the concrete warm on the soles of my feet and the water cool on their tops, the idle pleasure of directing the jet of water at leaves blown into the yard from the neighbouring houses and the dusty muck that accumulates out of air that seems to be falling down all around me rather than just filling up the space everything's in, even the stuff that's not here anymore.

There's an aircraft's vapour trail creeping across the blue sky, cicadas are creaking somewhere over by the back fence, on the nearest neighbour's deck which overlooks our back lawn with its carefully patterned lines of close mowing there's a loud lunch getting under way with clinking glasses and skiting about overseas travel, over the fence the paediatrician's wife is yelling 'Christufuh!' at her sullen son belting something with a stick, and Martin Klepka chucks the warm dregs of his glass of beer on to the freshly mown lawn and gets to his feet with a saucy hitch of his scrotum back into his shorts.

'Time for a nap!' says my father with his particular kind of relish and walks past his own grinning reflection in the French doors and into the darkness inside his house. She's old, in profile her head tilts back a bit as if to compensate for the heavy droop of her big eyelids, her large nose follows their downward plane as does the deep crease that runs down her cheek from the inner corner of her eye and under her neat chin. There's a small dewlap there but I can still see the elegance of her young neck. Her hair is a thick tangle of white and silver and half of a surprisingly large ear shows from under it. I see from the uprightness of her head that her back is straight, as it always was, and her mouth with its long top lip and sad chevron shape is open in speech or to yawn. She's wearing a simple pale blue woollen cardigan with a ribbed collar folded up under the back of her hair. When she turns around the cardigan's gone and I see the breasts of a young woman who has had babies, they are full with large dark nipples but lean apart from each other on the bony frame of her chest beneath wide shoulders. The yawn of speech is for me but I can't hear it and though I want so much to get closer to her I can't make my body move. Hers rocks towards me and away as if encouraging me to try harder. Her tongue comes in and out as if pushing the words towards me. I've seen this before. Sandy's beard is grey and clipped short with a silly shave line under his chin. He's crying and turning away from the bed, no, he doesn't want to help clean her. Then we're in a train moving along inside a mountain with many layers of tracks in complicated networks on top of and under each other. It's the movement of the train that's rocking my old mother's young breasts towards me and away again but it's also her urging me to make more effort, which I can't. I hear her yawning voice from time to time when the train moves between one noisy tunnel and another but the words are slowed down into a grinding, echoing, incomprehensible bass. Her tongue goes in and out. The heavy droop of her eyelids means she's looking down at her own breasts as if to make them the subject of her groaning sounds. Then there are green fields outside the train window, they're moving along beside us at the same speed as the train, we don't pass the landscape, we travel inside it. My father is there outside the train window next to which my mother is once again sitting in profile, her pale blue cardigan up under the silver curls at her neck, her sad mouth still talking silently. She's not looking at her husband's crazy grin turned towards us where he's pushing a mower along a neat grass strip that seems to be attached to the train. Then I see it's not a mower he's pushing it's his own big cock that my mother's not looking at, it's her averted profile I see even though I'm facing her, she's not going to look out the window where Marty's waving and waving with one hand while the other hand steers his dick. When we go back into the tunnels he disappears and many stations pass the train's windows. I'm facing my mother again but this time she's covered up and her eyelids have lifted. Her dark eyes are looking not at me but at the space between us and her mouth is making words I can't hear. Where's Sandy? He didn't come back. Then at last I rock forward into the place where she's sitting, I've succeeded, I'm going to be completely where she is, but she's not there anymore. We're at a station but I can't see her out the window, she's gone, and I need to pee, I need to pee so badly that I start to.

The little blueys always leave a foul bitter taste in your mouth but this time it's worse than usual and my tongue's sore as if I've bitten it. There's plenty of cold beer in the fridge but I stick my mouth under the bathroom handbasin tap instead and sluice the foulness out. Then I stand and piss into the toilet for a long time, it's slow these days, while the dream image of Marty's madly grinning face outside the train window and glimpses of my old-young mother break up and re-form as I turn the TV on and get the racing channel. Then I dress in clean underwear and a fresh shirt while the clock ticks down to 5.45. The odds have hauled in a bit but I'm still looking at something like thirty grand in take-home.

Some more or less horizontal rain is whacking against the glass doors to the deck and I push a towel from the bathroom against the leak-that-can't-be-fixed there. Marty was defiantly proud of the design flaws in his house, the results he said of uncompromising experiment, which was bullshit. They were the results of bad design, period. There are places on the outside walls where the oxide streaks have almost integrated themselves into the reddish character of the place. Inside, some of Marty's vaunted double-glazed windows can't shut properly anymore. I have to stuff the cracks with builder's bog and keep them closed. There's a spindly tree that's blocked one of the guttering downpipes by growing up it and erecting a small, optimistic baldachin of leaves at the top. It looks more like a creature than a plant. It doesn't go away, i.e. die. The grey moss patches on the southern wall are matched inside by shadows of mould, especially in rooms where the windows no longer open.

This dark mould began to appear in the months after

Marty died. It spooked me then but was just the result of Agnes sacking the housekeeper, even though she had a little boy. I remember the girl trudging down the hill from our house as I was coming up it. She had her boy by the hand—he was yelling blue murder. She turned her head over her shoulder and said something but I couldn't hear it.

Now these mould patterns look like the wraiths I had a thing about during my Kraftwerk phase. I shaved my hair off and wore an orange vinyl coat to wind my father up, which was also why I played *Ralf und Florian* at full volume. This had nothing to do with rebellion. I liked the music and the coat but I also liked Marty's inventive ways of objecting. Once he opened my bedroom door and hurled a bucketful of cold water at me. We stood opposite each other screaming with laughter, though I was the only one who was wet. He enjoyed these clashes, as he enjoyed denying me the seaward position when we stretched our legs.

'Nazi shit!' he would yell. He meant Kraftwerk as well as Somes Island.

He also complained when Agnes played Victoria de los angeles singing Canteloube's *Chants d'Auvergne*.

'Coucou-coucou!' He turned his hands into stubby wings and flapped out of the room. 'Folklorsick shit!'

My mother ignored him.

She often sat in the big downstairs room with a glass of wine, reading a book and listening to music. Her responsibility in the business was the textiles. The drapes and furniture coverings in the house were Klepka showpieces. After she sacked the housekeeper the place wasn't aired or cleaned much and the curtains in the upstairs rooms began to turn black. She took them all outside and burned them in the incinerator. She chucked a lot of other stuff in there too, Marty's mostly. If I'm haunted by anything it's the memory of Agnes standing straight-backed by the forty-four-gallon drum of the incinerator, her head tilted to watch the flakes of burning fabric and paper lift and scatter over the neighbourhood.

That's not true, about the haunting. Though all the upstairs rooms are empty now the one that Marty and Agnes slept in is emptier than the others. This is because it's the biggest room and therefore has more emptiness in it. But it's also because so much used to fill it. Not stuff, there wasn't much of that. It's them, Marty and Agnes. There was so much of *them*. Now they're gone there's so much not-them.

The face in the bathroom mirror has awful teeth in it, it hurts to brush them. Stranger are the tear tracks that have overflowed the lines in the face and disappeared into its whiskers. Were they chalk and cheese, my mother and father? Was Marty the crazy obsessive and Agnes the sensible pragmatist? He got the work done and she never cleaned the house. Was he the desperate prankster who sometimes made her scream? I don't remember her screaming often. I remember the tilt of her already greying head as the glowing fabric ash floated away across the dark bulk of Mount Victoria.

Trouble with my teeth is, the same cash prize that will fix them will buy what makes me grind them. About the time we flagged our sibling discussions about trust funds Sandy lectured me that the stuff used to be known as 'Hitler's drug'. That's the kind of useful information he's got at his fingertips. Vero didn't bat an eyelid. Back in the day she used to hide her jar of Obetrol from me. Now she's a Chardonnay matron in best Hawke's Bay style and her husband's a bottle-of-vodka a day moron. Pretty normal when you take the wide view. And Sandy?

Smitten students, he can't stop himself. The smug arsehole.

Racing steward's time.

I fill a tall glass with chilled India Pale Ale and take the first judicious mouthful. Next thing there's beer and broken glass all over the floor and I'm out the door.

Not much point asking me to check my coat nor if I'd like to 'take a bath', what about a spot of 'lovey dovey', don't think about it too hard, NB, or would that be Bushy Park this evening ('Not very funny, Micky . . .'). Never mind that 'Native Bush' always sounds like a bad joke nor that what she's up to is against the Honeysuckle's vague house rules. There's a beautiful cloud inside the pipe and I suck it back. NB gets the last bit for herself. The birdcage gate clangs open again high in my chest, they're racing, it's been a long, long day, but hey, shit, worth the wait. The weight, the wight.

'Jesus fucking Christ.'

'Don't talk bad like that, Mister Big Winner Micky-stick. Sticky-mick.'

'Be quiet,' I say and mean it. 'Just give me a minute. I need a minute or two.'

'Take all the time you want,' she says. She glows from head to foot, a tawny candle lit from within. 'No hurry, Micky.'

But here it comes, the speed gallop along the mesolimbic pathway. It's like a hard-on in the brain, let alone the one that springs out into the incensey fug of the room as NB wiggles my pants down.

'Ready to win big time, ride my horsey, what you say, Mick?'

'Whoa, steady,' I say.

'Whoa, whoa!'

'Ride 'em!' I'm going with the jockey thing, spur of the moment ha ha, as NB slides the condom on and lowers into the saddle.

'Micky, you're a big winner tonight!'

'Hot to trot!' I like NB but she won't understand why I'm suddenly weeping and laughing or laughing and weeping, can't tell. It's not the whorehouse patter, not winning the horse race, not the what-the-fuck look on the girl's face, not . . .

'Whassa matter, Micky, you okay baby?'

'I'm okay, I'm okay, don't fucking stop!'

'We're gonna win, Micky! Not stopping. You're the best . . .'

She doesn't know what I'm the best.

'Jockey!' I laugh sob, helping her out. 'Jockey!' The tears and snot's running down my face. 'The best jockey is what they're called, for fuck's sake!'

But NB's off me quick as a flash, pretty athletic when necessary, and wiping at my face with a wet towel, no mistaking her expression now. 'Enough, Micky, this is no good, you getting weird. You calm down now.'

. . . it's not, what?

I don't know.

'Or I call somebody.'

'I don't know what it is,' I say. I should be in heaven but I'm not. I should be triumphing but I don't give a shit. I'm trying not to laugh because it seems inappropriate but I don't know why. The speed is still making clods fly around the fast track that hooks my stiffy up to my brain.

Native Bush looks at it, the stiffy. 'You take it easy, all right, Micky?'

I lie back and we start again where we left off. I keep my eyes shut and let the girl unhalter me in a quiet paddock. It's just her job.

I took him to a lovely fresh grass paddock and he walked to one side and introduced himself to the horses in the adjoining paddock then introduced himself to the horses on the other side then mooched to the middle of the paddock and started grazing. He announced that he was in town and left it at that.

I hear Native Bush giving herself a sluice in the alcove.

'Let's leave it at that,' I say.

'Whatever you say, Micky.' Her hesitation says she cares about Michael Klepka a little bit. Just a little bit. At least I think so. Or she's scared. Enough to say, 'Maybe you take it easy, Micky. Know what I mean? No more yaha for a while, what you say?'

Then there's the way she's holding her dressing gown shut.

To my brother Sandy I say, I manage. Do you? I ration myself. Do you? There's a time and a place. What's yours you smug prick. Keeping in shape for you know what.

'Come on, NB, one more little toke. It's been a long day.' I mean one more bath, one more yaha, one more meow, call it what you like. I don't mean.

She knows what I don't mean.

'Come on, Micky, you know.'

I know.

'What's the matter, Micky? You so uptight. You gotta chill.'

I gotta chill.

These are *my* rules. She's a good kid.

'Did you ever,' I say, and stop. Her expression says, 'Me cunt you client.' Or it says, 'You wanna talk? Take me out for a nice dinner.' Or it says, 'Wanna get weird, the doorhandle wear your face.'

NB's face is a mirror I see myself in. The fear and anger are from me. The sadness is too. I put them in her face. What do I know about Native Bush? Not her real name, no kidding. She's got a daughter, Jessie. Real name, I've seen a cute cellphone picture. She's studying management at Massey. Her family back home think she works in hospitality. She doesn't like talking about herself. She does it to humour me but only a little bit. Jessie's hair's in sticking-up pigtails.

She's good at her job, Jessie's mother is.

'Did you ever,' I say, trying to drain my reflection out of her face, suck it back into me and seal the poison there, 'did you ever wonder what would happen if someone gave you a whole lot of money?'

'Money don't matter, Micky, no weird shit anyway.'

I'm still there, in her face. 'That's not what I'm talking about.'

'Like I said, you gotta chill. Or maybe time to go home.'

Time to go home. What will thirty grand-plus do to my life? Make it go on the same a bit longer. What will it do to NB's life?

'Micky, stop doing that!'

'Doing what?'

She points at her teeth.

'Listen,' I say, gritting mine. 'I'm going to give you a whole lot of money. A whole fucking lot. I'm collecting tomorrow. You listening? You don't have to do anything. Yes you do. You have to get the fuck out of here. Promise me.'

NB's a smart girl. What she's hearing is begging not threatening. Earlier in our evening the money thing was all fun and games.

'Mister Big Winner Micky-stick,' I remind her. 'Sticky-mick.'

She was lining up the door but now she stops. When she laughs my reflection flushes from her face. She stamps one bare foot on the floor. She's got one hand in front of her mouth to stop it being rude. The other hand's clutching her hair up as if to say, Good joke!

'What, you want me to come live in that stupid house?'

In the mirror of her face I see this weird old fucker.

The air outside is damp and there's a crack and fizz of blue ozone as a trolley bus accelerates out of the tunnel. I left my coat behind and the rain feels good soaking through my nice clean shirt. What the fuck was I thinking. Not what the silly little cunt thought I was. The dairy's still open and the kid's doing his homework. His moustache lifts automatically when he sees me but then shuts down again when he takes in how I look. That mirror thing. I get three big bars of chocolate from the rack, a milk chocolate with hazelnuts, a dark, and another with nuts and raisins.

My coat's up the hill with my wallet in it. Big decision time for the kid.

'Okay,' he says. 'Tomorrow. Morning.' My smokes are in the jacket too. 'Okay,' he says. His expression says, Does that mean you won't come in for your cigarettes tomorrow morning?

'Don't worry,' I say. 'It could be a lot worse. I could be asking for the till.' I smack the top of it. 'And a Bic, thanks.'

He hands me the lighter with an adult frown that's like a rehearsal for the future. For a moment I'm tempted to say, 'Did you even wonder what would happen if someone gave you a whole lot of money?' but I don't. Once is enough. Right now the natural order of things is fucking up. I'm standing in the rain jamming chocolate in my face and opening the cigarette packet at the same time.

I get a glimpse of the kid's face inside behind the counter and there I am again, reflected. This time what I see is just another regular nut-case from around here somewhere—the place is crawling with them and he's not going to be one of 'em, no sir, not likely, no way.

A few stoners are standing in the street outside a party at the tinnie house on the corner. A small girl in a big parka says, from inside the hood, 'No I'm not fuckin' going back in there you fuckin' ape.'

'That's the story,' I say, pushing past the guy. The girl's taking off down the hill.

'What did you say, cunt?'

But she'd turned her hooded head over her shoulder and said something that sounded like 'Luck of' but wasn't, so he's likely talking to her not me.

Up the hill. Back up the hill. How many times now?

Once when the housekeeper girl came down with her little boy yelling blue murder and yanking at her hand. He'd have been about six, funny little squirt, not quite right. She looked over her shoulder too and opened her mouth. She didn't have a hoodie on but her white face was small inside her dark hair.

What did she say?

Crunch of broken glass, smell of beer. I sweep the glass up thinking, movie? Then I decide, fuck channel. Then I re-decide movie. Then I mop the floor with a lemon scent. It's got to be Hitchcock. Fragments of glass glint in the sink. I chase them down the plughole. When Vero was little she believed the sparkle in sand at the beach was gold—you just had to take some home, you'd be rich. My hands under hot water tell me how cold the rest of me is. Hitchcock, *Rear Window.* That moment when you're inside Jeff's body and the window's his eyes. The whole world's out there. Each bit in its own little screen. In the mirror I'm putting a dry shirt on, back in the big room I'm turning on Marty's famous rectangular radiators, pure gold. *Gelt.* That look on NB's face. 'You want me to come live in that stupid house?'

This is the life.

Rear Window, 1954. One of Marty's favourites.

Stewart and Kelly. 'Big *schvantz*.' Marty's grin. I found out what he meant later.

Miss Lonelyhearts, Miss Torso, the loony songwriter playing the same tune over and over, the newlyweds pulling the blind up and down, the woman on the fire escape.

I organise a smoke on a bit of foil. I hold my hand out to watch the fingers shake. Then I get the Bic going. And a beer. The fuck channel. Big-arsed sheila taking it from behind. No good.

Rear Window.

The *voice on the radio.* 'Men, are you over forty? When you wake up in the morning, do you feel tired and rundown? Do you have that listless feeling?'

Always loved that bit.

Jeff trains his telescopic lens on Miss Torso.

Jeff trains the lens on the Theobalds having their argument.

Switch to the big-arsed sheila.

Switch back to Lisa: I'm not much on rear window ethics.

The big-arsed sheila, now she's giving herself a hand.

No good. Turn the TV off.

I get the last cake of chocolate and another beer.

Marty hated La-Z-Boys. Mine's a Dallas Power Recliner.

There's Marty on the grey screen, stuffing his face with chocolate and then tipping his recliner back. He looks older than I remember. I remember him filling the picnic hamper with glittery sand for Vero.

'We take the gold home, darlink!'

I remember him mowing the lawn at the back wearing a lampshade on his head. The housekeeper's little boy's sitting in the sun, watching. He's clapping and shrieking. Sometimes Marty let him push.

'You bastard,' Marty says on the screen. His face is lined and tired, with white bristles. It's me, out the rear window, in the mirror, I know, I know that. But it's him.

'What did that girl say?' he asks me.

'I don't know,' he says. 'I couldn't hear her.'

'I don't know, Marty,' I say, seeing myself say it. 'I couldn't hear her.'

Veronica

Can the sea have a different sound in winter? In summer it sounds blue, but now it sounds kind of grey-blue. Also, the seagulls along the Esplanade sound different too, more like winter, squawky and a bit bored, kind of overcast with arguments.

What you're going to say sometimes gets itself ready first as a thought, then as words, and then comes out as speech. Half the time what comes out as speech doesn't sound much like what you thought.

But it's true, the waves on the beach beyond the Promenade sound grey-blue—they have a darkish sound.

'Do you think sounds have colour?'

Nigel gives me a peeved look with pursed lips and even does a wee tut tut. He's a lovely man but he doesn't like to be interrupted. Mind you, he's not the only man I know who prefers to hold the megaphone. In between sucking big breaths into his walking rhythm, he's been going on and *on* about the new chef out at Mission. Apparently the Polenta Pasticciata alla Milanese is gorgeous and as good as anything you'd get in 'Milaano' with a long 'aa'. But, but!—if you're going to drink yourself to death you might as well do it in Hawke's Bay, right girls?

It's true the subject of drinking yourself to death anywhere isn't dear to my heart, but I didn't mean to be rude. Pat gives me a pert little 'Thanks!' look over Nigel's shoulder. She's going great guns. You'd hardly know we were into the full-bore block along by the Aquarium. Mind you, not an ounce on her, though the recent chin-job's left her looking a bit stretched around the chops.

On the other side of me Gwyn's not talking. All her reserves are for the next kilometre and then the chatty wind-down home. She's been a Volunteer the longest of us all, but she's packing it in before next Art Deco Weekend. She reckons there's only so many times you can listen to know-it-all Yanks from Miami, 'Art Deco capital of the wurrrld'. Or the ones from Santa Barbara who get it mixed up with Spanish Mission and you can't tell them. Besides which last year she got the Residential *and* the Garden Awards—she can retire 'job-well-done', and well deserved too. Her place is a sight for sore eyes.

But then she surprises us all. 'Synaesthesia,' she gasps. There's a film of sweat shining on her face and her tongue does a quick top-lip-wipe to get some of it. Nigel's head whips round and he opens his mouth as if to say something, but Gwyn gets in first. She's really working to keep the pace up. Walking next to her, I'm aware of the heat she's generating, you'd expect steam, there are big wet patches across the small of her back. 'It's when . . .'

'It's when,' starts Nigel.

'. . . it's when,' gasp, breathe, 'you experience one sense . . .'

'Oh shit,' says Nigel.

'. . . in terms of another, like . . .'

Nigel's stopped and is looking at his left arm.

'. . . like saying *a loud colour.*'

'Fuck,' says Nigel, and sinks to his knees on the footpath.

'Oh fuck.' His face has gone a funny puce colour. We've all stopped, and he's looking at us with his mouth open. Then his purple tongue comes out, he heaves in a huge rasping breath and falls on his face.

A whole lot of seagulls take off all at once, squawking like mad as if Nigel's frightened them, and just as I'm getting down on my knees beside him I see a rubbernecking driver in a white Mercedes do a giant swerve to miss a girl in a red puffer parka on the pedestrian crossing and a man on the footpath walk into a lamp-post outside the dairy because he was looking over at us too—he lets out an embarrassed bark of laughter.

Then everything seems to click back into place. Gwyn's got Nigel flipped on his side, but he's not breathing so we get him on his back and I start CPR. It's part of the Volunteer induction course though I've only ever practised on other Volunteers, with facecloths over their mouths. They teach us how to deal with chewing gum, a frequent choking hazard with the older Yanks. Pat's on her cellphone, I hear her giving the location very precisely and clearly: 'A—quar—i—um.' I have an inappropriate thought as I get my mouth over Nigel's and huff and puff into him before going back to the chest-pushing, which we Volunteers always practised to the rhythm of the Bee Gees' *Stayin' Alive*, push push push push, stayin' alive! The inappropriate thought is that Nigel must have had a big feed of that Polenta Pasticciata alla Milanese pretty recently with more than a few glasses of the Mission Reserve Syrah, knowing him, and I hope he doesn't throw up.

Even when she's next to a dying or possibly dead man and calling an ambulance on her cellphone, Pat's got the knack of standing just right with the knuckles of her left hand on her stuck-out hip.

Push push push push, stayin' alive!

Puffing, covering nose and mouth.

There's a small crowd, including the girl in the red parka. I can see the same expression on all their faces as I come up for another chest-push. It's a mixture of horror and curiosity.

'It's okay, thanks,' says Pat, as if responding to an offer of help. 'Unless anyone's a doctor?' she adds as an afterthought.

Then all at once something happens inside Nigel's body, like a tremor or a flinch inside him, and we get him on his side just as he burps out a big blob of dark stuff and then takes a massive breath. The red puffer girl comes forward and offers her parka.

'You need to keep him warm,' she says, and Pat says, 'Thanks, sweetie,' as if she's directing things.

Gwyn and I have a little tug of war to get the parka over Nigel. I'm trying to cover his legs but Gwyn's going for his top half. It ends up in the middle. Nigel's elderly shanks are sticking out from underneath—they're still tanned from his Italian foodie tour, and his face should be too, except that it's gone a nasty pale-khaki colour. Gwyn's got Nigel's head on her big thighs, which looks comfy.

Nigel seems to be staring at us but it's not clear if he's seeing anything. He's trying to hold his chest but can't get past the puffer jacket. Then he says 'Shit' in a funny, weak little voice, so unlike his normal one that Gwyn lets out a hoot of laughter, then covers her mouth. But it catches on—the rest of us can't help ourselves. Some of the watching crowd join in too, but most of them have begun to wander off. Pat's laugh is a kind of haw haw, which she lets go full volume for a while with her head chucked back, then shuts it down suddenly. I'm the last to stop—I think it's the relief—and Nigel's looking at me with what could be an annoyed expression, or just pain. The ambulance siren is closing in from the southern end of the Parade and the gulls, which had settled, all take off again with a great squawking.

'How are you, Nigel,' says Pat, getting down on one knee like a sprinter.

'Stupid bitch,' whispers Nigel, and closes his eyes.

Then the St John's guys are checking Nigel out and getting him on a stretcher with a blanket. The grey sound of the sea comes back now that the fuss has died down a bit, along with the smell of waves, a bit greyish too. One of the ambulance guys has the reddest beard I've ever seen, and the best teeth inside it. He keeps smiling at Nigel, who can't see him because he's got his eyes shut.

'Probably choked on his dinner,' suggests Pat, as if a bit miffed by what Nigel said to her.

'Heart attack, looks like,' says the smiling one. 'You ladies were brilliant. Saved your friend's life, I'd say.' He holds up the red puffer jacket. 'Whose is this?' The girl steps forward and claims it. She'd only had a tee-shirt on under it and her slender arms crossed over her chest are all goose-bumpy. 'Thank you, dear,' says the ambulance guy with the beard, and a wonderful blotchy pink blush rises all the way up the girl's neck and into her face.

'Let's get a move on,' says the other medic, who's got one of those shaved heads that men are going in for these days. Penis heads we call them among ourselves. Of course poor old Nigel's going all the way to Hastings, and now they're even knocking the Napier hospital down, shame on them.

'I'm going with him,' I say. 'Someone'll have to help with the details.'

Something strange has started to happen since we all had our laugh.

'Are you sure?' say Pat and Gwyn more or less in unison, meaning thank goodness.

I see them striding into the homeward leg as we do a u-turn and head for the Hastings highway. They're going flat out with their faces towards each other, talking at once. Their hair flounces up and down as if synchronised—push push push push!

All around them everything looks just the same as it was, but it's not.

It's well over forty years since Dad died, and I wouldn't have thought about him all that much since—maybe a bit for the first few years but not once my life got under way. We weren't the closest. But now, back he comes, thanks to Nigel. I was only sixteen when he had his heart attack. He was mowing the grass at the back of our place the neat way he did, and acting the goat in one way or another, wearing an apron but nothing else so his skinny bum or lack of it was exposed, or one of Mum's summer frocks or something silly on his head. It was always a performance. When we were all little, it was for us and we loved it, but later we found it stupid, his show-offy performances, so he stopped. But he started doing them again when the housekeeper came on Saturdays with her little boy. Her name was Pam and his was Sam. We called them Sampan and thought we were clever. Sandy started it—he had a huge row with Dad who called him a smart-arsed little shit. Can't argue with that. When the kid was really small he sat in his pushchair and clapped. Later on he'd sit on the edge of the deck and make weird crowing noises. We all knew he wasn't quite right, but Pam who did the house always brought him. When he was big enough to hold the stem of the mower's handle, Dad sometimes let him push too. He'd stagger forward between those long, hairy legs, screaming.

Before Sam arrived, Pam did the house on Fridays. But then it switched to weekends so we could mind Sam while his mum cleaned—it was just part of the family routine. Or maybe it was because of the performances.

When Dad had his heart attack he just went straight down on the lawn and never moved again. I was sitting with the boy, who let out a shriek of laughter at Dad's new trick. I remember Mum running out of the house in her styley underwear—she'd been getting changed after her nap. I haven't thought about this for years and years. With her clothes on she always looked chic, but without them she just looked little and thin. She was yelling at us to call the ambulance. Mick came out on the deck and then ran back inside to do it. Then he ran back out and jumped down to the lawn. Mum had turned Dad over, and she and Mick were on opposite sides of him. The neighbours with the overlooking balcony had been having loud lunch with clinky glasses and they were all standing there gawping down, drinks in hand. Mick screamed, 'What the fuck are you looking at!' He was sobbing, but Mum seemed quite calm, she was holding Dad's head. Pam came and grabbed the little boy and took him inside. He'd been laughing and clapping, but I heard him yelling inside the house. They'd gone by the time the ambulance arrived. Dad was dead, anyway. From the deck you could see where his neat lines of mowing stopped about a third of the way through the job—the dark stripes that went across in one direction, and the pale ones in the other. Dad's old wooden-handled push-mower was halfway along one of the dark stripes, and after the ambulance people took him away the mower just stayed there for a couple of days, with its handle sticking up. It looked a bit like Dad—skinny and practical, but also weird, a ghost. The gawking lunch neighbours had gone inside and shut their French doors, so the place was deserted, except for the mower standing up out there on its neat pattern. There was that nice smell of freshly mown grass, but as well the pooey pong of Sam, who'd filled his pants again.

'Friend of yours?' says the bearded ambulance driver, and Nigel's eyes open a little bit. They'd given him a shot of something, but he's not one to miss the conversation if it's about him.

'A very dear old friend,' I say, with my hand on Nigel's bony ankle. 'A special one.' I'd like to think it's a smile that twists Nigel's lips but it's more likely the pain in his chest. 'It's too bad we have to go all the way over to Hastings,' I say.

The ambulance guy's keeping an eye on Nigel, but he shows his teeth to me for a moment. 'Why?' he asks. The marvellous teeth are not necessarily smiling, it's the framing effect of his beard that makes them stand out the way they do. 'Do you think the old heap was worth keeping? He, I mean it, hasn't been any use for the better part of twenty years.'

I beg your pardon?

Then he turns back to Nigel, whose eyes have begun to flick between me and the medic. I realise that Red Beard recognises the former Director of the Art Deco Trust, so why would he want to start a smart-aleck conversation now, in his ambulance?

And, *old heap*? Looking at Nigel?

And why does it always have to be *the better part*?

I know my face has gone red, but I don't say anything. Even though the Napier hospital was built in 1969, and had nothing to do with the Art Deco Trust, Nigel was always in the news about it.

'Some things just go past their use-by date, don't you reckon?' says Red Beard. He's looking at Nigel, so it's hard to tell who he's talking to, or about, Nigel or me. I can't believe what I'm hearing.

I can imagine that Nigel's getting the full benefit of those teeth, the beard. I give his ankle a squeeze, just to mean don't pay any attention, *use-by date?*—but then I see his mouth make one of those twisty shapes, I swear he's looking straight at me, and it's a Nigel smile this time all right.

'What is it that some things always *just* go past?' he whispers, and winks. It's an old game we play, from one of Nigel's favourites, Flann O'Brien's 'Catechism of Clichés'.

'Their use-by date,' I say, and Red Beard's face whips round to look at me. The smile is there, but now I know it isn't. Nigel was never a supporter of the hospital as a heritage site, he thought the building was an utter shocker.

He only stood up for it because he thought there should be a hospital there, on the hill, close to the airport. It was freehold land, the city owned it, therefore the people of Napier did.

'Don't give rich pricks the view!' he'd yell at public meetings.

'My father was an architect,' I say, and Nigel rolls his eyes. I'm just trying to shift the conversation somewhere else more or less relevant but not so argumentative or distressing for Nigel. Then I add, 'Martin Klepka,' out of respect I suppose.

'Is that right?' Red Beard's smiling as if he's interested. He's looking straight at me now. 'A modern one?' he says, with even more of his teeth showing.

I can feel the heat in the roots of my hair. I can also see that bloody old Nigel's even enjoying this. He gives his head a little rock from side to side, as if to say, *Go on*!

'Depends what you mean by *modern*,' I say, well-briefed modern/moderne/modernist cultural heritage Volunteer to the fore.

I can tell that our friend Beardy's one of those people who were all for tearing down 'the old pile', and most of them also get agitated by all the attention paid to heritage buildings at the expense of amenities, such as support for St John's Ambulance in his case I imagine.

'Modern?' he says, still looking at me with those hard eyes above his 'smile'. I find I'm squeezing Nigel's ankle quite fiercely, and so I relax my grip. 'I suppose I mean, is it still any use to anybody?'

Nigel closes his eyes and gives his foot a little wiggle inside my hand, as if we're cheating at cards.

'My brother lives in one of Martin Klepka's houses,' I say, looking the rude bugger in the eye and feeling a *coup en passant* opportunity presenting itself. 'It's *alive*.'

'It's?' The teeth stay bared.

A nasty fart smell fills the back of the ambulance.

'Sorry.' Nigel's whisper's almost inaudible, and if you hadn't heard him earlier you wouldn't know his lips then make the little arse-puff shapes of 'Polenta Pasticciata'. But then he raises his voice above a whisper and says, 'Smells like something just died,' and twitches his foot in my hand again.

Always my best partner, dear man, but too unpredictable for bridge, and really he liked the chit-chat and trying to find ways to cheat more than the game.

Then we're in the ambulance bay by the Emergencies Department and Red Beard and Penis Head are getting Nigel on a gurney. His eyes are closed but I think he's pretending. The expression on his face is like the one he gets when he's looking at an object or a building he really doesn't like.

'Oh *dear!*' he'll say any minute now, but of course he doesn't, and all at once I'm terrified he's going to die right here, in this pale corridor that smells of floor cleaner, instead of in somewhere like Mil-aa-no, or out at the dear old Mission vineyard, eating the food he loves and having a few glasses of wine and a gossip. Or sitting on the little terrace of his nice unit with its big planters of blue-flowered rosemary for the bees, in summer, that is—please let Nigel have another summer here, when the sound of the sea is that chalky blue again, and the sound of the cards being shuffled is like little turquoise waves falling on the pebbles.

Off he's going at a fair clip, pushed along by an orderly, and Penis Head puts his hand on my arm as I'm about to follow. Red Beard's banging the rear door of the ambulance shut again. He's not smiling anymore or whatever it was his teeth were doing inside that gross hedge.

'Get a cup of coffee, mate,' says Penis Head. He's quite shiny and smells a bit like bergamot. 'The triage nurse has to check your friend out. I mean in, sorry.' His whole head goes beetroot-red. His hand turns me firmly in the direction of the café. 'I'll tell them where to find you,' he says, quite kindly. But then he adds, 'If you're needed.'

Hospitals are places where everyone has a job to do except the patients and people waiting to see them—the doers and the hopers. The girl by the till in the café seems to be stranded somewhere between the two—it takes her a while to see me, even though I'm standing in front of her. It's only nine in the morning and already she looks as though it's time to go home. But then, maybe she's been on a night shift. I want to tell her that she should unbutton the top of her uniform and ease the pressure there, then I realise it's me that's feeling cramped up.

'How far have you come?' she asks, checking out my walking gear.

'From Napier,' I say, without thinking. Then I hear myself and laugh, expecting the girl to get the joke, but she doesn't. 'In an ambulance,' I say, knowing I'm about to start crying because of the laugh, and then I do. 'With a friend,' I say. 'He had a heart attack.'

The girl's got the loveliest complexion, old-fashioned peaches and cream, and the most beautiful big blue eyes that she's spoiled with too much mascara. Her hair's lovely, too, the palest of amber, and it matches a little spray of freckles across her cheeks. All at once that not-quite-here look disappears from her face and she comes around the counter and puts a big soft arm around my shoulders.

'Just take it easy, girl,' she says. 'I'll bring you a cup of tea.' Then she does something quite wonderful. She knows that I'm going to say I haven't got any money with me, so she gets in first. 'Don't worry about paying now,' she says. 'You'll be in visiting your friend before you know it.'

She finds me a table by the window and goes back to the counter, only to return with some paper napkins for me to mop up with. She gives me a pat on the hand. She's got a big diamond engagement ring on her marriage finger and a greenstone one on her thumb. Her nails have coral-pink nail polish with that glitter stuff included. It's like she's trying to work out how to be whoever she is.

How can some people be so kind and others so mean? What I can't tell the lovely girl is that I wasn't with my mother when she died. I felt so useless, just like now, nothing I could *do*, only that was well over twenty years ago while I was in Venice where the Italian side of Mum's family came from, with wee Sophie, who was too young to know how to deal with me when we got the news about her gran.

'Hang in there, girl,' the girl says. I'm sixty-two and she's, what, twenty at a pinch.

I'm off sugar but when the girl brings me my cup I put two good teaspoons in. The strong sweet stuff reaches all the way back to that misty place where a couple of old wooden jetty bollards gripped together by a black iron band with a length of orange rope hung over a rusty hook on the side stood up in front of the grey silk moiré expanse of sea with the towers and cupolas of Venice disappearing in the distance. It was all so clear, even though it was misty. I was seeing everything at once. The smell of the sea wasn't quite fresh, nor was it unpleasant, it was just like the atmosphere, like breath after sleep. Sophie ran down after me from the hotel and found me by the edge of the grey breathing water. Of course it was evening back home and morning over where we were. Mick and Sandy had waited until they knew I'd be up before they made the phone call. I loved the sweet pistachio ice cream they had in Venice, and the morning pastries with shaved almonds and lemon icing, and the little coffees that a teaspoon of sugar thickened. I still had the taste of the morning pastry in my mouth where my tears were running into its corners. She was only seventy, my lovely little mother. I wasn't there, and what was worse, she wasn't here in Venice where she'd always said she'd take us one day.

First Dad, now Mum.

The lovely girl comes and sits down with me. 'How's it going?' she says. 'I'm off now, done the early opener. You going to be okay?'

'I'm fine,' I say. 'You get a bit of a shock, is all. It's brought back a few memories.'

'Like what?' she says.

'Go home,' I say. I pick up her hand, the one with the big diamond engagement ring on it. 'He's a lucky young man,' I say.

She leans in close with those big blue over-mascaraed eyes. 'He's the sun, moon and stars,' she says. She gives my hand a squeeze. 'And he makes me yell my head off, if you know what I mean. Luck-y me.'

I watch her tired bottom push out through the cafeteria doors—her hem's pulled round a bit crooked, the backs of her flatties are trodden down, and it's only then that I notice one leg's slightly withered and she walks with a bit of a gimp. But her hair catches the neon in the corridor and she turns the corner like a sunrise.

Because of that one thin leg next to the other nicely rounded one, the girl is like two people trying to work out how to be together in the same life-body. It's not real to say you love someone you've only met across a café counter, but I feel choking love for the kind girl with the sun-moon-and-stars fiancé, mostly because I hope she'll work out how to be a whole person. So far she's making a good job of it.

Isn't that what we're here for—to 'take care'? Isn't that what the Volunteers are doing? What the hospital's doing? What the ambulance jokers are doing, even that smart-aleck Red Beard with the smile-that-isn't? What Mum and Dad were doing for Sampan years ago?

After Sandy broke the news on the phone he said, 'She should have been there,' and then stopped. There was a continuous crackling noise on the line as if the words he'd said were scraping themselves through a tunnel towards me. 'She . . . there.' What did he mean? The words scraped through me, they cut me in half, I couldn't work out if I was the 'she' who should have been 'there' with Mum, or if the 'she' was Mum who should have been 'there' with me and her granddaughter Sophie.

'What do you mean?' I said. I had to push the words past a great swelling in my throat. The polite hotel man who'd called me from the dining room to the phone was tidying things on the reception counter and chatting to the young woman there, who was looking at him with a flirty you've-got-to-be-kidding expression. The man was very handsome and sleek, with the kind of skin tone that makes a white shirt look special, but he had the longest eyelashes which he was lowering with a quiver, and he was making a pout with his mouth, as a result of which he looked like a dick. The world just beyond me didn't connect with where I was. 'Do you mean I should have been there?'

'No, Vero,' Sandy said patiently, 'though that would have been good. I mean, she'd have loved to be where you are.' Even then he had that fruity voice that makes you feel talked down to.

'When she died?' I waited a moment. 'She'd have loved to die in Venice?'

There was another long pause during which, as well as the crackling, I could hear those weird noises Sandy makes with his throat when he's on the phone. Then they stopped.

'Just let us know if you need a hand with anything.' That was Mick's voice, flat and a bit raspy as usual. 'Just get on back here kiddo and take care of yourself.' Then he hung up.

Unless he's angry, you can never tell how Mick feels about anything from the sound of his voice. He might as well be talking over his shoulder to the pump attendant at a service station, saying something like, 'Fill her up, regular,' as he walks inside to the cashier to buy some smokes as well. But I like Mick's voice a whole lot better than Sandy's. Back then, what Mick had to say was fine: come home, *take care*. The only trouble was, I still couldn't sort out the 'She . . . there' thing. Plus I was angry. Then I felt Sophie's little head on my chest. I could smell the hotel shampoo in her hair, something a bit cinnamony, or maybe that was what they'd sprinkled on her morning hot chocolate. She was crying too. The poor kid was only nine going on ten. She still has that lovely fresh parting in her crazy hair, though it's got a tiny bit of grey in it now.

'Nanna should have been *here*,' she said, though she hadn't heard the phone conversation with Sandy. 'She'd have loved to be here with us.'

Then things got back into focus, *here*. Of course it was simple. But Sandy's words had made a little rip in me, they'd torn something. I'm feeling it again in the cafeteria where a few people with no job to do except hope are sitting around waiting for the moment when that might change, when they might be taking care of someone besides themselves.

Get on back here and take care of yourself.

Or did he mean, *Take care of yourself and get on back here*?

Not that it matters.

He's a total ratbag, Micky, but at least you know where you are with him. Trouble is he doesn't have a clue where he is with himself. Except perhaps in the place he likes to jeer at—the 'haunted house'. His smoker's laugh.

How can you forgive a father for putting that kind of a hold on one of his kids?

It seems I'm 'not needed' at the hospital after all, says the crisp girl at Reception who's busy watering a potted palm with a little pink, long-spouted watering-can like a toy surgical implement—'Thanks for your patience, Mrs?'—but I don't bother to leave my name, and when the taxi driver tries to make sympathetic conversation it's as though time has sped up and his words are gone before I can shape my mouth around an appropriate reply.

When I get home and go inside for money to pay for the taxi, Pete's sitting at the kitchen table looking pretty much as I'd expected he would. Those blue eyes spoiled with pink, and a fair bit of blotchiness around the cheeks. He lifts his cup of coffee to his lips as if to delay what he has to say, which will be an apology. His lips quiver down to the hot coffee, and his cup's none too steady either.

I find my purse and go out to the taxi before he can speak. When I come back he's got to his feet and prepared his speech.

'You all right, Ver? What's up? You're pretty late.'

Me late?

I can't be bothered with what I know's coming next. Pete's got his charming puppy look on.

'I'm fine,' I say, before he can begin to find an elaborate way of saying he's sorry without meaning it. 'Nigel conked out by the Aquarium. I went with him to the hospital.'

'Jesus,' he says. 'How is the poor old . . . ?'

'Believe it or not he looks a lot better than you right now, Peter.' *Peter* is none-too-subtle code for shut up. When you've been together for thirty-seven years, you don't need to spell such things out anymore.

Pete sits back down at the kitchen table with his coffee. I feel like saying, 'So I don't imagine you'll be getting in to work today,' but I don't (a) because he never does after a bender, and (b) because then he'd have to explain that he's feeling stressed about the business, he just lost the plot for a moment, and he's very sorry, won't happen again (in brackets, for a while anyway). Oh, and (c) we needed to rethink the business model (in brackets, in the bar at the

Waiohiki Golf Club and, presumably, somewhere else for the rest of the night after they shut around six-thirtyish).

The Asians stopped coming to the Bay after 2008, the Germans don't want to look at Art Deco buildings, the Americans always know better, the gannets are only interesting for half the year and three of those months are the dud season, there's only two variations on a vineyard visit (drink/don't drink), and look! Here comes the firm's Co-Director, CEO and Marketing Manager, Peter 'Bullseye' Dartworth! Responding swiftly to yesterday's fully expected phone call from the bank re cashflow and loan repayments with an urgently scheduled strategic meeting!

Shut up, Veronica! I say to the niggly voice in my head. Next thing it'll start telling me all about what happened, when I wasn't even there.

When the Co-Director and Accounts Manager wasn't even there.

Shut up.

Pete's in the spare room ensuite having a shower when I go out. He's acting blasé by singing Van Morrison's 'Moondance' in that nice karaoke impersonation voice he's still got, and for a moment I want to go back in and either blow him a kiss through the steam and tell him not to worry, we'll sort the business out, it was only a shot across the bows from the bank—or.

The *or* makes my heart do a giant thump, and something puffed-up rises into my throat. There's a flush over my whole body, the like of which hasn't happened for a few years.

Or *what*?

I get into the car and sit there pointing down the driveway at the road with my hands on the steering wheel. Then I have to wipe the perspiration off my top lip, so I get a tissue from the glove-box.

Or tell Peter about the fling I had in Venice back when Sophie and I went, the year Mum died, twenty-six years ago.

'Twenty-six years,' I say to the steering wheel, not with the making-it-up voice in my head, but with my own real voice, the one that tells the truth. Maybe now's the time.

Poor old Pete, says the voice in my head.

'Bugger poor old Pete,' I say aloud, and start the car. Poor old Pete's a damn fine salesman, he could sell wooden leg liniment as they say—he sold himself to me good and proper and no complaints then, and no complaints about Sophie, none about the fun times, which were many and lasted a while. But now the talent's been pissed away and the charm's something he has to tune up in the shower, where he's probably taking a leak down the plughole at the same time.

What makes people worth preserving?

The flip-side of that question is, What makes people worth calling in the wreckers to? When they're 'past their use-by date'?

It comes to me quickly, then, as if the thought's been waiting quietly outside for me to answer the door. Of course I knew the thought was there. It's been there for a while but I wasn't quite ready for it.

It is: I can use my share of the Klepka Trust funds to buy Pete out. Then he can wreck himself if he wants to. But I'm not bailing the company out while he's still pissing down its plughole. No matter how often he edges that suggestion carefully across the table at me, with his winning look. The full sensation in my throat and chest is still there—the *or* thing—and it's why the door's open now for my Plan A to walk in and for Pete to walk out if he wants to.

I open the door in my mind and watch what happens again.

I tell Pete about Venice, he does something or not, I buy him out of Bay Tours, I rebuild the business, or not, but I don't chuck my only free capital at it while he's clinging on.

Maybe it's past its use-by date, ha ha.

Something like fresh air or sunshine comes in.

Who's opened the door—in fact, who's also just entered with neat, confident steps, the click of good leather shoes (a sexy sound), along with Plan A, is the man who said, in the hotel lift, with a courteous hand on the small of my back, 'You don't haff to if you don't want to,' and, 'I'm sorry about the cigar. We Chermans.' But I did *haff to*, and the cigar was fine.

Frankie looks up from her computer as I walk in and says, 'Goodness me, Veronica!' She pushes her glasses down her nose and gives me the once-over with those eyes that know how to keep looking patiently at the same old customer questions ('How long does the tour take?' 'An afternoon.' It's in the brochure, read the fucking thing). 'You're looking refreshed,' she says, a bit archly.

Actually, it didn't take an afternoon, it took a fair bit of a night, while Sophie was asleep, I hope, in our room a couple of doors along.

'It was poor old Nigel,' I say, daring Frankie to push her luck. 'He had a heart attack. Along by the Aquarium.' Frankie looks a bit crushed. 'And Peter won't be in today,' I say. 'He's indisposed.'

'Ah,' says Frankie, and goes back to her computer. 'Coffee's hot,' she adds, as if turning a switch to normal. And then, as if it doesn't really matter, 'Is the old faggot okay?'

'No help required, apparently,' I say, somehow associating that information with the little pink plastic watering-can at Reception.

I sit down to check my emails and there, like a row of spoiled brats, are no fewer than six red-flagged messages from my big brother Sandy. They'll all be the same, each with a *trying again* sigh attached. I sit looking at them. Even the cigar taste on—I haven't heard my inside voice say the name for a good long time. Even the cigar taste on *Ulrich's*—Uli's—mouth was nice, and so was the way he carefully inserted two of his perfectly manicured art conservator's fingers in my cunt.

My *cunt*.

His nice jokes about handling works of art with care. I liked that.

I also liked it when there was little enough careful handling later on.

I open the first of Sandy's emails and see the word MICK'S in capital letters. I go to the last one and there it is again, MICK'S. I know perfectly well that he wants Micky to move out so the house can be sold, and I know why, too.

I think MICK'S gone off the rails. He rang me.

MICK was never *on* rails, Sandy, you moron. Nor was Mick.

There's nothing more from the bank.

'I'm having lunch with Soph,' I say to Frankie. 'Something's up.'

'Never a dull moment,' says Frankie, and waits.

'Listen,' I say.

'It's okay, Veronica,' she says. 'I can read the tea leaves, too.'

'Can you let me know if the bank calls again?'

'They won't,' she says. 'They got the red-flag call in before the long weekend, then they all buggered off. You won't hear again till the middle of next week. Plenty of time.'

My first thought is, How blessed I am to have someone like Frankie on the team.

My second thought is, But there's never been plenty of time.

I hardly even notice that I'm walking around the block to the Middle Eastern restaurant.

'Was I wanted, Mum?' asks Soph. She's got her grandfather's acetylene eyes that just go on looking at you. But her grandmother's lovely olive complexion. And her mad hair.

'Oh, Soph!' I say. 'Don't tell me!'

'Are you nuts?' she says, still looking. 'Not me, for God's sake. Angie, Mum. *Wee Ange*.'

So, we got *there* smartly. It's what happens when you know each other as well as me and my daughter.

'Bloody hell,' I say. 'How far?'

'Three months.'

We're eating falafels, which I don't like, but I'm supporting Soph who's gone vego in support of her daughter, my granddaughter, *wee Ange*, Angie, Angela, how could she be!

'She's asking, Mum. You know. *Was I wanted.*'

I push my falafels away. They seem at once oily and dry. Everything that's happening today involves conflict of one kind or another. Sophie's still looking at me without shifting her direction—it's 'the look' all over again, the one that Dad used to freak us out with, though he didn't know he was doing it.

'As if it makes any difference,' I say.

'I know, Mum. But you try telling a seventeen-year-old that. Everything's black and white.' She pauses and smiles at me from under those eyes. She's thirty-seven and we both know that for seventeen years it hasn't mattered whether Angela was 'wanted' or not. There's a line of grey along the lovely middle parting in the mad hair Sophie got from her grandmother, and the voice inside me that writes other people's scripts for them says, *Old enough to be a grandmother.*

'Back in the day we used to call them shotguns,' I say. 'I was out-to-here with you in my wedding dress. Pete was irresistible, he was the most fun of anyone I'd ever met, and to say you *weren't wanted* would be like saying I never wanted him. Never wanted to root him. But I did, and no regrets.'

'Settle down, Mum,' says my daughter. 'No need to get into the sordid details.' Then, at last, she drops her eyes. 'Can't really say the same about Angie's dad, the wanker.'

'But it didn't make any difference, did it?' I say to the grandmother-to-be in front of me who has half a falafel on her fork and a dab of hummus in the corner of her mouth.

She shakes her head, still not looking. Then I see the

tears plopping into her plate. 'She's only a little kid!' she says, as if she'd rather be shouting.

I reach across the table with my serviette and dab the hummus away from her lips, which are shaking.

'Sorry,' she says.

'No you're not, Soph,' I say. 'Any more than you were when you saw Angie for the first time, mostly covered in white goo, with a face the colour of a radish. It was love at first sight. I'll bet you weren't thinking about the wanker then. And you were what, nineteen?'

'Twenty,' says Sophie. 'Fully paid-up adult, eh.' Then she heaves a great big sigh, mops her eyes with her paper table napkin and blows her nose into it. Then she puts it on her plate.

'Are you quite finished?' I say. 'You're disgusting.'

That nice crooked smile of hers. God almighty, we could all have had different lives, but what's the point of wandering around in that 'if only' no-hoper paddock?

'I know what you're going to say, but you don't need to say it. Just nod your head if I'm right,' she says. I nod. 'Not yet,' snaps my daughter, whose sense of humour is only one of the things I love about her. 'You're going to say that of course Angie's body's her own and she's got the right to make her own decisions about it and the life she's going to live in it, but what I need to do is give her a reason to believe I'd like her to have the baby, even if I don't, because that's the only way she'll give herself half a chance to accept that *she* does, if she does, and it's only fear.'

There's a pause while I unravel Soph's blurt, which has all the marks of a thought that's been going around and around in her head until it's a complete tangle, like the hair that's sitting on top of it.

'Well?' she says, boring in with the eyes.

I nod. It wouldn't be fair for me to start crying now, so I don't, though at this particular moment I'd like nothing better than to grab Sophie and give us both the excuse to have a bloody great big sooky hug-and-howl together.

'You want to hear the good part?'

I nod again.

'He's a Frenchman in the vineyard supply business from, wait for it, Tonnellerie Rousseau Père et Fils.' Sophie makes a point of giving the French words her best pouty pronunciation, which is legit. 'The poor girl thinks she'll go to France with him. She told me his joke about the vibrating sorting table. I wonder how many times he's told that one. Oh, and he's married. With kids. And he's about forty.'

'And you want to kill him,' I say.

'No, I don't,' says Soph. 'I want my daughter to kick him in the nuts and tell him he'll have to sell quite a few more fucking wine barrels for the next few years.'

'Does she really believe this guy?'

'Mum, she's seventeen. So was I, once. So were you. That wasn't the right question.'

'None of us knew what that was, did we? The right question,' I say. 'But look—here we are.'

There's a silence while we look at each other. The Pam part of Sampan was a solo mum too, not much older than me then. They're always with us, the Pams—in fact, in some ways they are us. Sampan was almost adopted family, for a while.

'Vibrating sorting table,' I say. 'It's a more complex industry than I'd thought.'

'Thanks, Mum.' My daughter has a wonderful laugh that's always finished with a gurgle at the back of her throat. She's a toughie when it comes to it, and she's been a great mother. 'Well, all hands to the pump, probably.'

'Or not,' I say. 'It's not *your* hopes you need to be getting up.'

She gives me a grin. 'Got the last word, as usual,' she says. 'I'll let you know how it goes. Angie may want to have a wise old woman chat.'

'Any time,' I say. And here come those words again. 'And you take care of yourself, too.'

'You too, Mum.' Her cellphone rings and she looks at her watch. She runs the office at Nelson Park Primary School. 'Back to the front line.' She waggles the phone at me.

'I know, I know,' I say. 'I should.'

She comes around the table and pushes her face into my neck. 'Love you, Mum,' she says, and I want to say, 'Love you too, Soph,' but I can't without losing it, so I pull her face into my neck and hold it there. She lets me keep her for as long as I like while her warm breath puffs down the front of my blouse onto my breast.

Then she's going out the door into the sunshine. She moves just like my Sophie. She still has the same forward momentum as the kid who took her first steps at Tangoio beach and fell flat on her face in the sand and looked up laughing through her crazy sandy curls and her mouthful of grit. The kid who wouldn't be told no when she was learning to swim and ended up swallowing so much water she chucked up a whole lot of carrots and stuff and they had to evacuate the kids' pool and drain it. The high-school kid who stormed out when Pete told her she wasn't to, though he always went off and charmed his way into whatever dodgy situation she needed to be fished out of at two in the morning, and probably had a couple of drinks or a joint while he was there, to give him credit. The girl who looked me in the eye and said she was pregnant to 'some dick'. The one who's turning left and is marching with quick strides to where her car's parked. She's my best friend, she's my baby, she's my big girl, she's probably a grandmother-in-waiting. How could anyone be so fucked up—*Fucked. Up.*—as to have any use for a term like 'past its use-by date'?

The sunshine looks good out there, bright enough to show up the rhythmic smears of glass-cleaning on the street-front window, and I think it might be nice to go over to the Promenade and see what colour the water is now, and what colour sound it's making, but I'm not quite ready to stand up.

The restaurant owner comes over to clear our plates away, and asks a bit anxiously if we're finished. Neither of us has eaten much.

'Yes thank you, George,' I say. 'It was very nice, thank you.' Then I say, 'I'd like a glass of wine, please.'

Soph and I have lunch here quite often, couple of times a week—I'm familiar with the thumbed menus, the fly-spotted tourism posters of the Roman ruins at Baalbeck, and the sound of George's wife alternately complaining and singing in the background, it's hard to tell the difference and it probably doesn't matter. But I've never asked for a glass of wine before, let alone after finishing my lunch.

The man looks at me with a little smile. He's got a lot of

black hair growing out of his ears and nostrils, and Soph's joke about it is that his bum must look like a curry-combed stallion's.

'Something to celebrate?' he asks.

'Oh Yes,' I say, with a capital Y, and mean it.

'You're an old hippie,' Soph had said over her shoulder as she left, and I know she intended it as a compliment of sorts. But really, does what I'm feeling belong anywhere or at any time in particular? Or to anyone? I know George's name because we've chatted, I know he's Palestinian and an Orthodox Christian, and I know both his and his wife's families were originally from Galilee, which I associate with the Christmas crèche Micky used to vandalise enthusiastically on our atheist father's behalf when we were at Clyde Quay Primary School in Wellington, but I realise I don't know if he and his wife have kids or grandchildren, let alone great-grandchildren, or if they like living in Napier, or even why they're here.

'Would you like to try a glass of Lebanese wine, or would you prefer Hawke's Bay?' asks George in his polite way, but the impression I'm getting is that he thinks the situation calls for something special.

'Lebanese,' I say. 'I don't think I've ever had the pleasure. A red wine, if possible.'

'Chateau Musar,' says George. 'They also make a good arak.'

What pisses me off about Sandy is that his work at the university up in Auckland's all about different cultures and what makes them tick, as he never tires of reminding us, but the furthest he ever gets with that in the real world is the scenic bits of his female foreign students. And, just lately, how he can buy one of them by booting Mick out of the house, unless I'm much mistaken.

George brings me the glass of wine, and I see his wife standing between the kitchen and the counter with a big smile on her face. She gives me a wave.

'My wife thinks you will have a new grandchild,' says George. 'Is it true?'

'Yes,' I say, raising the glass to her. 'Maybe.' I have to pause for a second before I correct myself. 'Great-grandchild,' I say, almost not believing it myself.

'We have six,' says George, who looks about fifty, max. 'Only grandchildren! But the parents don't want to cook.'

'In that case, George,' I say, 'you don't have the inheritance thing to worry about.'

'They already have all of it,' he says, as if what I'd just said wasn't a joke. And maybe it wasn't.

There's only one lunch table still in action. George's wife is hovering, and I don't know her name.

'Why don't you both have a glass of wine with me,' I say. 'I feel a bit strange sitting here drinking all by myself, and anyway.'

'And anyway!' says George—I notice back rows of gold teeth. He waves to his wife, a beckoning sign with two fingers together.

It's the first time I've seen the woman this side of the counter, and my first thought is, what an amazing beauty she must have been. She has a long face and, though the skin around her eyes is hatched with fine lines, there's no grey in the dark hair that's pulled back behind her ears. She walks towards me with the stoop of someone who's worked long hours, but then straightens after she puts two more glasses on the table, and holds out her arms. She's tall, and her invitation to embrace is made with her arms in a semi-circle, gracefully, like a ballet dancer, with her head on one side. Then I see how very beautiful she *is.* I stand up, and she kisses me on both cheeks and says something like *ma-brook.* There's a hint of thyme on her breath.

'I'm Ruth,' she says.

'I'm Veronica.'

'Veron-ica.' She repeats the name carefully, nodding her head. 'It's a beautiful name.' She pauses, and seems to try a smile, a question-smile, unlike the one from the kitchen door. 'Like the saint. With the wiping.'

So—filling in the outlines. Little bit odd. I neither agree nor disagree about the saintliness.

Sometimes it's impossible to tell the difference between manners and feeling, and maybe sometimes there isn't any.

Then we sit and clink glasses. A great-grandchild? My day seems to have piled up behind me and the pressure of it's pushing a babble of words out, goodness knows how many are making sense. And yes, they know of Nigel, and their children were all born in the old hospital before it closed, will he be all right?

But a great-grandchild! The only one?

I step around the possibility that wee Ange may make up her own mind about that. Both George and Ruth have tiny gold crosses around their necks, and there was the Catholicky Saint Veronica moment.

'Yes,' I say. 'Incredible.' We all take another sip. I try to manufacture a laugh around 'great grandmother', but it doesn't work, not naturally, anyway. George gets up and sorts out the last lunch bill. Then he swings the 'closed' sign around on the restaurant's door.

'It's okay,' he says, 'you are not a hostage!'—and I see his wife wince. Not just my attempted jokes, then.

'And you?' I say. 'Six? Grandchildren?' We go on stumbling over the generation thing. 'How is that possible? Two young people like you.'

'But you know, the present is very short,' says Ruth. She holds up her wine glass—only a half, barely sipped. 'We have wine in Lebanon three thousand years before Jesus Christ. So, maybe five thousand years now. Here only since Mission—what, maybe one hundred years?'

Her husband is shaking his head, and I'm shaking mine too, but on the inside, without moving it. I'm waiting to see where this is going. With any luck, not far.

Ruth puts her hand on mine. It's warm, and dry, and just a little rough. There's a fresh sticking-plaster around her little finger. The nails are trimmed short, and she has a very thin gold wedding band on her marriage finger.

'Here, everybody is young, like the wine,' she says. 'Even the beautiful *old* people, like us.' Her mouth makes a small, twisting grimace on the word 'old'. Then it smiles again, but with irony, or sadness. She takes a decent mouthful of her wine. As the swallow flexes her long throat, she tips her head back and closes her eyes. Her eyelashes quiver against her cheeks. Then she opens her eyes very wide and gives my hand a pat. 'And thank you for the help. For the Nablus.'

I'm thinking Ruth may be a bit crazy.

The Nablus Middle Eastern Restaurant is one of the recommendeds on Bay Tours brochures ('Good value for money, authentic Middle Eastern, vegetarian dishes a speciality'), and I'm getting that, as well as being crazy, Ruth may be the brains and George the gold-filled smile here. But the brochure's not why we're having the glass of wine, and it's not entirely why she's thanking me, of all people.

'So why *Nablus*?' I ask, hoping to steer us away from time and age, and the quiver in Ruth's eyelashes.

'You know,' she says, 'both our families came to Lebanon in 1948. From Palestine.' George makes a tisk-tisk sound and puts his hand on her cheek, which she matches with a hand against his neck—those long fingers, pushing up into his hair. Their touching is intimate but as if they hardly know they're doing it. 'From Nablus,' she says, turning her mouth against his palm.

Now I'm understanding that this is really the grandchildren story against a historical backdrop, as well as a performance about a marriage filled with small restraining gestures.

'But then you came here why?' I feel as though I'm reading one of those autocue things.

'So, George was born in Lebanon in 1962, me a little later.' She smiles, modestly. 'I was younger.' The eyelashes. 'A girl.'

'In Bekaa,' says George. 'Both families.' Now she's covered George's hand on her cheek with hers. I seem to be perving on a secret story told by their little physical intimacies. 'Where the wine is.'

'Yes, in Bekaa,' says Ruth. They're both looking at me while their intimate little hand-play continues. I've heard of Bekaa and its wine, but that's not what the hands are telling me about.

'George's family comes to New Zealand when he is two, a baby. When he is twenty-two, his father sends him back to Lebanon.' Again, the modest smile.

'And the rest is history, as they say'—I say—but like my earlier quip about inheritance this one doesn't get much purchase.

'Her father is my father's oldest friend,' says George. 'I have to bring his daughter away from the civil war. Unfortunately, she is very beautiful. It's a disaster!'

'He was my hero,' says Ruth. She takes George's hand from her cheek and returns it gently to his lap.

'And then I am her husband, a little later.' George seems to be hurrying the story along. 'We had three kids, girls. The first grandson four years ago. Two more two years ago, a boy and a girl. Three this year, girls.' He's taking little glances at Ruth. 'The invasion!'

The gap opened by his wife's silence isn't hard to find.

'And your family?' I ask her.

Her gaze is simple and straightforward, though one eye has a very slight cast in it, so that she seems to be looking both at me and past me.

'They were killed,' she says, 'in the Bekaa. In the war.' And before I can butt in with an 'I'm so sorry,' or something, she puts one hand on her husband's arm—these little gestures they have—and raises her glass. 'So . . .'

I pick up my cue.

'Here's to the grandchildren,' I say. And add, 'The invasion.' It seems a bit much to add the great-grandchild.

'The grandchildren,' we say in a ragged unison. George tops us up, and we clink glasses again and drink. The wine's not bad, southern Rhoneish style, a bit thin at the end.

Now doesn't seem like the right moment to comment on it. There's still two or three glasses left in the bottle, but George and his wife get up from the table. Again, that look both direct and askance, and the kisses on both cheeks that are both polite and with feeling. Then Ruth walks back around the counter to the kitchen, stooping again by the time she goes in there.

'That must have been terrible,' I say to George. 'I mean, your wife's family. Ruth's family.'

'Terrible, yes,' he says. 'Her three brothers. That's why we had three. But they are daughters.' He's standing with two empty glasses and the quarter-full bottle in his hands. He shrugs, lifting the bottle and glasses. 'But . . .'

'Life goes on,' I say, feeling as if I've been prompted again. Then I sit looking out the window with a mouthful of the wine left in my glass. I can hear Ruth and George busy in the kitchen, and their voices, not loud, but firm with each other, speaking in what I guess must be Arabic, not disagreeing, but discussing. Then George comes back and reverses the 'closed' sign on the door.

'Life goes on, as you see,' he says, with his front-of-house smile back.

I should get going, but I don't. I don't quite know why I should, or where to. Someone puts on Middle Eastern music in the kitchen. No more customers come in. After a little while, George brings me a small gritty coffee, a piece of sweet baklava and an arak, 'on the house'. The arak turns white when he adds water, and tastes like cough medicine, and it's only after I've knocked it back that I realise how strong it is.

When I get to the waterfront, the sea has that chalky

blue colour that I've often thought was just right for the town's best plastered façades, a limey kind of turquoise. Now I couldn't give a shit what it might be good for except waves. It's just lovely, it's a smooth, calm kind of sound. That's all I need at the moment. Little pale-blue whispers of waves.

What in God's name was I thinking, 'Here's to the invasion!' Stupid cow that I am. It reminds me of when Dad would stare down any attempt to do the family history thing.

But then, maybe it didn't matter. In the bigger scheme of things. And George said it first.

The park bench isn't all that comfortable. If you sit right back in it the edge cuts into your thighs, and if you sit forward you get a crick in your back. Someone's idea of traditional. I sit right back, since I won't be staying long. My knees are squarish in my jeans, and I don't have the elongated thighs I could tell were under Ruth's dress. Mum, though quite petite, had the long thighs, and Dad's were like furry beanpoles. Mine must be a throwback to something or other. Someone or other. Between them I can line up an organised view across a strip of scruffy beige grass, the worn asphalt footpath, the grey pebbly beach, the whiteness of the gently dropping little waves, the soupy turquoise of the sea, and then a shining stretch-marked expanse of blue-grey water out to the horizon. Above that it's too bright, like light reflected off tinfoil, and I feel a headache coming on.

It's not exactly warm, but I sit there anyway, paralysing my short thighs, to clear my head before picking up the car from the office. Thinking about Plan A+. Plan A+, the new one that has a great-grandchild in it. Then I push myself up off the awkward bench.

Why don't you use a cellphone, Pete's always wanting to know. Along with Frankie and my own daughter. Because that's why we're paying Frankie to sit behind a desk with a phone on it during working hours. And because I hate them. And here's another reason: the answerphone at home's blinking madly, and the caller numbers are all the same. Sandy's. There's only one reason I can think of, and it's that he's finally decided to throw himself under the wheels of a student young enough to be his granddaughter. Under the thighs of.

There are signs of a scrupulous clean-up in the kitchen, dishes all put away, and there are fresh flowers in a vase, white and yellow chrysanthemums from the corner dairy—I noticed a black plastic bucket of them outside there on the way into town—and next to them a message from Pete on the Bay Tours jotter pad.

'I've booked us dinner at the Mission. Don't make plans! X Peter'

Peter, mind you.

Plans.

And besides which, are you going to charge it to the company?

There's still sunlight in the sunporch and plenty of light from the sea view out to the east, but it won't be long, couple of hours at the most, before that strange light-change happens out there, when the sun gets low in the west and a kind of reflection warms the eastern sea horizon for a little while before evening. Nigel ribs me about living up on the hill with 'the rich pricks', fat chance, but most of the garden's his idea, completely seasonal, lots of perennials and a succession of changing annual colours. Our chrysanthemums are the tough little perennial sub-shrubs—Nigel considers the florists' versions to be vulgar, the old snob. They're what Pete's bought from the dairy, as if he hadn't noticed what was before his eyes in the garden.

But anyway.

When I wake up again I know I've had a dream about Ulrich, but all I remember is that he was seconded to the European Institute of Design in Venice, which almost certainly wasn't in the dream *anyway*, but which was how our careful conversation started in the hotel bar. He could well have been one of the most boring people I ever met, and he could have made a habit of picking up single foreign women in bars. But my dream isn't telling me anything now it's over. I've got some dried spit on my cheek, and a taste of aniseed in my mouth from the arak back at the Nablus. It's getting twilighty, that little reflected flush of sunset across at the horizon has gone, the porch is chilly, and I walk through the unlit house along a track that's in my brain, not on the floor, whose creaks seem to follow me.

I go past the phone with its blinking lights and upstairs for a shower. I'll have a listen to the last message when I go back down. Pete comes in whistling in that aimless, meandering way men do when they're feeling vulnerable—sometimes the older ones do it while they're waiting for attention at the Bay Tours counter.

The older ones.

The whistling stops when I turn the shower on, but

Pete doesn't come upstairs to say hello through the steam. I let the shampoo run over me until all the bright, winking bubbles have stopped swirling around my feet. Then I get out and stand in front of the full-length mirror.

I look at my body. It's misty, or rather the mirror is. Some little rivulets run down the mirror over the tummy-fold that's there now, under which he carefully inserted his art conservator's fingers twenty-six years ago when it wasn't. After the cigars there was another smell, it was on his body not his breath, it was like overlays of old-fashioned men's cologne and the hot, starchy hotel laundry service, and under that, which was good for a start, a simple animal smell, warm skin, a day's work, a few whiskeys, whatever was trapped in his big deep armpits, around the creases where his black pubic hair shaded off into a pale furze across his thighs, and around his ears, where there was a slight sweetness, as if he'd been rubbing his thoughtful temples with fingers scented by beeswax.

He didn't mind that I didn't have long thighs, like beautiful tired Ruth at the Nablus, or probably like the student Sandy's panting after. No, he liked Veronica Dartsworth—or Veronica Klepka, the untraceable name I gave him—just the way she was, cuddly, with big tits he pushed his face into. He pushed his face into the pillow next to my head when he came for the last time, and let go of my wrists, and cursed in German. *Scheisse!* I knew it was cursing, because after a while he apologised, *I'm so sorry, I don't want it to be finished, aber das ist Alles.*

Scheisse!

There's no more.

And then it was the next morning.

Solemn wee Sophie and I went for ages on the vaporetto around all the stops on the way to the airport, which was besieged by tourists going in both directions. Mum's funeral in Wellington felt like an extension of that. Swarms of people were arriving and leaving at the house. Nasty little rain squalls were chasing sunshine across Dad's famous windows. Mick's eyes had disappeared into his head, and Sandy had a flash new suit one size too small. Mick got completely pissed and wandered off into the rain, and Sandy made a rather good speech of thanks. Then the red house emptied. There was a ringing sound in it, as if the walls were vibrating. There was furniture everywhere, but all the drapes had been replaced by wooden venetian blinds that clattered in the wind because Sandy insisted on 'letting some air in', a chattering that went on after dark when everyone had left. Sophie took me by the hand, and we went upstairs and slept together through most of the next day in my old room—she took up so little space I needed to find her sometimes and feel her breath on my neck again. Pete was staying in a hotel. The only impression I had of him after we got back from Venice was the uncertain tremor of his smile and the banal smell of his aftershave. By the time I saw him again late on the day after the funeral, the sweet smell of beeswax around Ulrich's ears had gone down into the place where it's remained now for twenty-six years.

I sit on the side of our bed to strap my watch on, holding it against my knee, something I'll do most days, often more than once, same old watch, different time, but now it feels strange, as if I'm seeing myself do something new and unusual. The time feels strange too, getting on for six in the evening, when I'd often enough be sitting where I am now, 'on my side of the bed', putting my watch on again after a shower, hearing Pete downstairs switching on the six o'clock news, yelling up to me, 'Want to see all the shitty stuff that's happening?'

Only he's not yelling out tonight, though I can hear him moving around down there, and 'my side of the bed' has been all there is for a while. I've hardly even noticed how often Pete's been using the one in the spare room. There's a book on the/my bedside table—it's Kate Atkinson's *Case Histories* with the private investigator Jackson Brodie—and my spare reading glasses. I've been quite enjoying it. I like the sense I get of the writer—she must be fun, it seems to me, as a person. Though she's a bit Englishy, and I don't imagine she'd have any difficulty making her thoughts move swiftly into words and then into interesting conversation.

I don't know what I'm going to do, but I'm about to do it.

My brain shifts down a gear, and I think, I don't imagine Kate Atkinson has this kind of difficulty.

Anyway.

Pete does an exaggerated double-take when I come into the living room in my jeans and a sweater. He's got his nice Donegal jacket on and looks a lot better than he did this morning—for example, shaved and combed, his shirt freshly pressed from the dry-cleaners.

'So, casual attire this evening, is it?' For a moment it looks as though he's going to close the gap between us and give me a hug, but then he stops. 'Oh, come on, Ver,' he says. Must be my expression or something. 'Come on, sweetie, let's just go out and have a nice meal, then we can talk things over.'

'I'd rather do it now, if you don't mind, Pete,' I say, and hear myself sounding like a crabby old bitch, so I add, 'but thanks for the flowers.'

Shouldn't that have been, '*And* thanks for the flowers?'

He's not putting on an act when he holds his head in his hands and lets out a growl. 'Okay,' he says, and sits at the dining table. 'Where do you want to start? My drinking problem, the fucked business or the fact that the place needs new wallpaper again?' I still love the man, but it's wearing thin when he adds, 'Or is there *something else*?' in his best sarcastic tone.

'Angie's pregnant,' I say. Knowing the moment I open my mouth to say it that Ulrich may have to stay where he's been all this time.

Pete's jaw drops, he jumps up, knocking the chair away, his face goes red, and I see him battle to get a word in ahead of his stutter—he chokes on the sound of rage or pain that had just started to come out.

'I had lunch with Soph,' I say. 'It's okay—the poor kid wasn't raped or anything, you don't have to go tearing around somewhere and knock the boy's teeth in.'

Plan B+.

It's pathetic, but I feel a great thump of disappointment, of anticlimax, land on me heavily, sadly, knocking the breath out of me.

So this is what I'm going to do.

Pete sits down again and gets his faculties under control.

'She's a *kid*,' he says. 'Wee Ange. She's *s-s-s-seventeen*!' He's not going to be able to manage it, the speech thing.

His eyes have filled up with tears.

'Yes, seventeen,' I say. 'So not really a kid. She's going to have to think about it. But she'll probably do it. She'll be needing us.'

There's a squeal of brakes and a car horn held down for too long out in the street, and some teenage macho shouting, and Pete startles as if he's had an electric shock. He's blinking at his tears, but I see the thought *She'll be needing us* go into his system like a calming drug, so that he smiles next, that lovely straight smile across his face that makes his cheeks crinkle.

'She'll be needing us,' he says without difficulty. The smile stays there. 'Yes. So who is the lucky little prick?'

'It's a forty-year-old Frenchman,' I say. 'He sells wine barrels.'

'You're kidding.' Pete's smile twitches back and forth between amusement and horror.

'No I'm not,' I say, knowing I'm going to play the good-humour card next, and hating myself for it. 'And vibrating sorting tables.'

'And *what*?'

'Vibrating sorting tables. Tools of the trade, apparently.' I feel a bit sick, all at once, with the horrible dishonesty of it, and Pete's face is struggling to work out what to do about all this. Am I taking the piss out of him? (Well, am I?)

The man I've loved one way or another for ten years longer than I've kept the German's beeswaxy aroma to myself doesn't really have secrets, or the ability to keep them. He gives things his best shot, which isn't always too accurate, it's true. He's a likes-a-laugh fellow who's most at ease with a drink in his hand, in the company of other men, telling blokey fibs. Or playing with his daughter and then his granddaughter at the beach, tripping up first one and then, twenty-something years later, the other, chucking first one and then the other into the little turquoise waves, first when he had the hard body of a not-bad number eleven with a wicked sidestep, next when his body was a bit stringy, though with a wee drinker's paunch. But always laughing while doing the chucking or tripping-up, the laugh that could outsmart his stutter better than anything else, the laugh that could sidestep the traps in his life.

Haven't heard the Pete laugh for a while.

'Well, fuck me,' he says, and he's laughing now. 'A Froggie great-grandchild. What would the odds be.' A few months back, before the balance sheet started leaning the wrong way, he'd have considered this a good enough reason to pour us a drink. Not tonight. 'Life,' he says. 'What a bitch.'

I'd laugh too, it seems the best thing to do under the circumstances, but I can't. It rises up again, *There's something I need to tell you*, but I can't do that either. It's well and truly gone now.

'So,' I say. 'Plan B time, probably.'

But not that one.

'Guess so,' Pete says, with his eyebrows up, and the fact that he doesn't ask what Plan A might have consisted of suggests rather strongly that he thinks it would have involved recapitalising Bay Tours with Klepka Trust funds. The laughter, Pete's laughter, is winding down into a silence which he swerves past, or sidesteps, let's say, with some of the grace and flair of old when he stands up in his nice speckled grey Donegal jacket, still a tall, handsome man, with that straight-line grin on his face, and says, 'Come on, Ver, let's . . .'—as the phone rings.

We're looking at each other across the table, him standing and me still sitting down, with a strange unfamiliar weight like my own body pressing my thighs on the rim of the seat, and Pete's grin gets stuck in place as the good will drains away from it. At the moment I get up to answer the phone, knowing who it's going to be, I see what I've seen thousands of times in our life together—that Pete likes things to be simple, the way they were a moment ago, for just long enough to get a laugh started. But things never are simple, so he'll cut a move, and before long will be chasing his laugh into company where talking's easy and what's best is always the next punch line, and the Pete who's in the thick of it will be a character he's become for the time being, perfectly believable, especially to Pete, but never quite the same as the one before or the next one, the next Pete 'Bullseye'.

There's a gap between the moment when Pete's smile goes stiff and me lifting my own weight away from the edge of the chair that's more like a space-gap than a time one—a kind of surface, stopped for the moment, in which the details of my husband's face are clearly printed. For a start there's the smile, which made my throat feel furry back in the day and was even known to get me wet. Now it's got the same optimism, but not for as long on any given occasion, and it's self-conscious about the teeth that used to be its confident come-hitherers. The laugh-lines that used to spread out like ripples in water from the corners of Pete's mouth have done what such lines do, and deepened into trenches that don't go away but run down either side of his mouth like crossing-out marks against the smile. Of course his face still has those handsome bones in it, especially the long ones under his chin and the ones that lift his eyes above the flat planes of his rather too-smooth cheeks, but now the cheeks have a boozer's purple scribblings all over them, and his morning shave often leaves little patches of white missed-that-bit bristle. The scar he got above his left eyebrow from a sprig-raking when he played for the Bay forty years ago has gone a funny purple colour, and stands out under the eyebrow that never quite covered it up and that now grows outwards with long, stiff, curly white hairs. His ears are bigger than they used to be.

His eyes stay on me for a while, still blue in spite of the drink, determined in their way, and the smile stays there for a while too, but then both the gaze and the smile just fade away into his departure, at which point space gives way to time and I'm reaching for the phone before it switches to voice-message.

I have a strange thought in this time-space between the sound of my husband opening the door to go out—doing so quite gently, as if taking care not to disrupt my phone call—and me reaching for the phone. It's that what I read in those signs written by life on my husband's face should remain mysterious. I shouldn't pretend that I know how to read their detail. The world he lives in, and how it's written all over the face I've known for forty-odd years, are still mysteries to me. That's the way it should be. We should go on being unknown to each other, otherwise there's nothing to know, and what would be the point of living with someone who's no more mysterious than the News at Six, on the dot, day after day?

Pete's car drives off, which is how I think of it, rather than Pete drives off in his car. I hope the silly bugger doesn't get pissed again and turn the vibrating sorting table into his joke-of-the-night. He will, though. I hope he leaves his car and gets a taxi home, whatever else he does.

In a way he's like my father, or perhaps that's just to say he's like men. Dad didn't particularly like me, even though he loved me, but he gave me his best shot—as when he collected sand with 'gold' in it to take home long after I'd stopped believing it was gold. I never told him I'd stopped believing, and he never behaved as if I had. I think he knew, but it was a routine we kept doing together, like a ritual.

Pete, on the other hand, likes me even if he doesn't really love me. But who knows.

'Christ all-bloody mighty, Veronica, where have you been!'

Good question, Sandy, but here I am, holding the phone away from my ear as usual with you.

'Here I am,' I say. 'What's up?'

Pete's face, of all faces, should tell a story—for example, the story of the day that started when he had one too many at the golf club yesterday evening and that may extend into two days if he does it again, and of course the story of the life that banks up behind that drink. But his face doesn't tell stories, it's just patterns, like the sea in different weather from one day to the next, from one time of day to the next.

'Vero! Veronica! Are you there?'

Here, there.

You can't *read* Pete, there's no tour guide to his life.

Sandy, however.

'What's going on, Vero? Fuck's sake. Are you okay? Did you listen to my messages? Have you heard?'

'Heard what?'

Sandy's breathing is really noisy, there's a lot of damp air going in and out of him the way it does when he rings from the gym. But he's not ringing from the gym. This time it just goes on and on, then there's some rustling noises, he says, 'Hang on!' in a funny desperate way, unlike Sandy—so's the swearing for that matter—and then there's a clatter, the breathing stops, but he says, 'Fuck!' in the distance. Then the breathing's back and a car door slams.

'Sorry, dropped the phone paying the taxi, Mick's dead Vero!'

Sandy's words are packed in tight and I don't get them. 'What?' I say, trying to prise them apart.

'I'm just getting a plane down. Mick's dead. Some girl found him at home, Vero.'

A noise like the breathy wheeze of bus air-brakes, a car horn tooting.

'He was sitting in front of the TV but it wasn't even turned on.'

I walk through to the kitchen and sit down at the table. Pete's chrysanthemums are there in their vase but he didn't put any water in it.

'What girl?' I say. I take the vase over to the sink and turn the tap on to fill it.

'Vero, for Christ's sake, what are you doing?'

'I'm putting water in a vase,' I say to what becomes a long silence with Sandy's laboured breathing in it, and the far-off noise of the airport terminal. 'Sorry, Sandy,' I say. 'Just give me a minute.' I put the phone down and get the vase full, then take it back to the table. Then I retrieve the phone and sit down just as Sandy's words, *Mick's dead*, thump me in the chest.

'She was returning his coat,' says Sandy. 'He'd left it at her place.' He's got his calm-and-in-control voice back. 'There's nothing fishy about it,' he says. 'The girl called the police. Mick just died, Vero.' He does some of his throat clicks. 'I'm so sorry. You really loved the mad bugger, didn't you?'

I can't get the words organised to talk with, and anyway, all at once I hate the sound of Sandy's voice being calm and sympathetic.

But then they come. 'What do you mean, I really loved the mad bugger? Didn't you, you sanctimonious piece of shit? He was your brother too.'

A pause. Sandy's breathing has gone away. As if in the far distance are the sounds of business, of crowds, of many voices, some thin tinny music, a public announcements ding-dong.

'Sorry, Sandy,' I say. 'Yes, I did love him. Sorry, I didn't mean that. What I just said.'

'Well, good for you, Veronica,' says my oldest brother, enunciating precisely, 'because I didn't. I couldn't stand him. He was a total arsehole, and he just got worse. So why don't you get your fat arse down to Wellington first thing in the morning and help me sort all the shit he's left behind out, sort out all the shit he's left behind.'

Poor old Sandy, just has to get it right. He hangs up, or whatever you do with cellphones—his makes a thick, wet click—and then I'm left with the soft hiss of my phone where it lies on the table, as if what we've just said to each other is being smoothed over or erased, and then some beeps, all those voice-messages that Sandy sent throughout the afternoon. Poor old fucked-up Micky, he did get worse and worse, and my heart will break soon, partly because I'm not really surprised by the news that he's died, but now I just need to mark out what I know.

The first voice-message from Sandy must have come about the time I was having lunch with Sophie. Sandy's emails at work were from last night. So some time between when Sandy got it into his head that Mick was going 'off the rails' yesterday, and when the girl found him sitting dead in front of his TV before lunch today, my mad brother, the one who could never get further from the house he grew up in than the end of Oriental Bay, who used to pinch my diet pills and not even bother to lie about it, whose flat, harsh voice was a comfort to me whenever I heard it, which was seldom—some time in that space, probably when everyone else was asleep, Michael Klepka turned himself off, just like the TV he and Dad used to watch movies on together all the time in the year or two before Dad died, and there they sat, not seeing each other.

I go to the fridge and get the bottle of Mission Reserve Chardonnay that Pete's been careful not to open. Mick didn't drink wine, he always drank beer, but I don't, so tough luck, Mick. I pour a good-sized glass of the wine and wonder if it was oaked in a Tonnellerie Père et Fils cask. He'd have enjoyed the story, even though he had no time for the kids.

'Ah well, Micky,' I say, as the tears start, how many times is that, my God, what a day. 'You mad old bugger. At least you're out of that fucking house at last.' I lift the glass to my dead brother and find myself toasting the big bunch of dumb, well-meaning dairy-bucket chrysanthemums at head height directly in front of me. 'You too. Bloody hopeless, the pair of you.'

It's very good wine, and it's good to have the cry I couldn't while I was with Soph in the Nablus, but both the glass of wine and the tears are soon finished. It's like I'm celebrating something, which is all wrong but doesn't feel that way.

When I was a kid I loved the way the car's headlights would make a tunnel in the darkness that we went on and on through, that seemed to open up ahead of us all the way to the concrete back wall of the garage at the red house. On the back wall Dad had painted in big red letters, DON'T STOP! He used to sneak the car slowly towards the back wall until the headlights were almost touching while we kids all shrieked *Don't stop, don't stop!*—but then at the last minute he would. Part of the fun was just doing it over and over, every time we came home. Then, of course, he stopped doing it, because we were older, but the big red letters stayed there, getting stained with mould and the water that leaked down the wall from the shonky terrace above. Once, a couple of years before Dad died, Micky drove the car into the back wall. He was about sixteen, he'd just got his licence. We heard the noise and ran down. The two of them were sitting in the car screaming with laughter and punching at each other.

I go to the hospital cafeteria first, to see if the lovely girl's there, but she's not. I explain to the one who is that I owe them for a cup of tea this morning, and the woman looks at me as if I'm crazy, which I probably seem. Then I go to Reception and ask for Nigel's ward, and the woman there rolls her eyes and says, 'Not another one!'

I hear the sound of voices and laughter before I get to the two-bed bay where Nigel's propped up holding court. His white hair's sticking up in a tuft so he looks like a galah with his beaky nose pointed at the ceiling and a loud cackle coming out of the wide open mouth underneath it. When he sees me he reels back in mock horror.

'That woman was kissing me when I came to!' he hisses. 'And that was: Came. To.' He glares around the room. 'Tee-with-just-one-oh, came to my senses.' Nigel has an assortment of tubes attached to his body, and machines parked next to him. 'Don't come *near* me,' he says. 'They went in. I've got a brand new *stent*.'

There are half a dozen of Nigel's mates parked around the bed, as well as three hospital staff. Pat and Gwyn are there, I can identify their flowers among the assortment in the room—Pat's is an extravagant boutique arrangement with fern leaves, and Gwyn's a big assortment of autumn dahlias, salvias, asters and tibouchinas from her garden. It occurs to me I could have brought the chrysanthemums, except that Nigel would have disliked them and said, 'Oh *dear.* You shouldn't have.' There are a couple more Volunteers, including the vintage-car nut Vincent, who's got his Art Deco Weekend straw boater on. The bloke who looks after catering at the Mission's there, he's known as Soda for some reason, and Nigel's pal Duds, who goes on foodie tours with him. In the next bed there's a pretty crook-looking old chap with the hopeful smile of a new chum plastered on his face.

'Let me introduce you, Veronica,' says Nigel. 'You

know the riff-raff, but these are the people who pulled me through. This young man is my namesake Nigel, we all call him Nige but don't try that with me, he's the Gas Passer or, if you must, the anaesthetist. Thanks to Nige I hardly noticed what they were doing to me. This lovely young thing is Doctor Emanuelle from Venezuela, she does hearts and she's not really twenty years old. This kind soul is Patty, not to be confused with Pat here, she's my Florence Nightingale, she can't wait for you all to go so she can clean me up again. And this distinguished gentleman,' says Nigel, wincing as he makes a grand gesture towards the new chum in the next bed, 'is Mr Harvey Bristol, known to his friends as Cream, I believe, who for many years gave good advice to the Port Authority—most of which they ignored, to their shame, isn't that right, Cream?'

'Too true,' says Mr Bristol, and goes back to the smile.

Nigel's looking at me with eyes that have filled with tears. 'Come here, sweetheart,' he says, holding out his arms, one of which has a tube attached to it. We hug, carefully. He's got a sourish, antiseptic hospital smell, and awful breath, so I plant a kiss on his forehead and accept the chair Dr Emanuelle has pushed towards me. 'You really did save my life, Veronica. *Saved. My. Life*! She did, didn't she? Everyone says you were abso-lutely magnificent.'

'Yes, she must have been,' says the too-young cardiologist with an exotic accent. 'But soon, you will need to rest, Nigel, or we have to do it all over again. Good night, everybody.'

'Buenas noces, Doctor,' says Nigel. The foodie tour before last was Spain. 'Ven a visitarme cuantas veces quiras.'

The young anaesthetist Nige waves at the room and gets

halfway out following the sexy Venezuelan laughter before Nigel calls after him, 'What autumnal precipitation will I soon be as right as, Doctor?'

'Rain!' we all shout before the poor guy gets his head around what's going on.

'And what is it that I'll be out of here in, other than a coffin?'

'No time flat!' says the young man, quick as a flash.

'So they don't call you Nigel for nothing, or rather, *sin razón*,' says Nigel. 'Go on, get out of here, I've heard you practising your Spanish on her. This place is a filthy den of lust.' He looks around at us. 'My dear friends,' he says. 'And I include you, Patty, my angel nurse, and you, sir, my companion in pain. How wonderful life is. Especially when it . . . ?'

'Goes on,' we say.

'And we're all boxes not of you-know-what but . . . ?'

'Birds.'

'And especially when you'll be what, exactly, in no time at all, darling?' says Gwyn, an old hand at our game.

The *ghost of* a smile. Why do we say that?

'Oh, Gwyneth, my dearest green-fingered one,' sighs Nigel, falling back against his pillows and closing his eyes. 'My old self, darling. My *old* self. Of course that's what I'll be, more's the pity.'

Sandy

‘So—what brings you to the nut house, Professor?’ she said, in that way that fairly fluent German speakers of English have, at once very correct and colloquial, but also odd, so that you can’t quite tell if they’re joking or not. ‘I didn’t know you interested yourself in nuts. I thought your speciality was Plattdeutsch poetry?’ She smiled nicely and politely, and held her hand out for me to shake. ‘I heard your lecture, Professor Klepka, it was quite interesting.’

Quite interesting.

Since we were in the Tropische Nutzpflanzen glasshouse at the botanical gardens near the university, I began to assume that humour wasn’t her intention, but then she said, still holding my hand at once politely and a little too long, ‘Unless, that is, you consider Klaus Groth to have been a “nut case”?’

And so it began—the not very good jokes that were flirtatious, not in a sexual way, but as youthful challenges to my sense of my own importance and the importance of the Plattdeutsch poet Klaus Groth, not a very sexy topic, any more than my lecture about him and Johannes Brahms was; but then also in a sexual way, because the jokes were inviting me, a married man of fifty-nine, a scholar, a keynote speaker, to play, to frolic, to be inappropriate.

The young woman’s straight, dark hair was pulled back quite severely behind her ears, and she even looked a little like the local Dahlem film-star legend Brigitte Horney, famous for her singing role in the 1934 classic *Love, Death and the Devil*, so I let my hand retain its polite hold on hers as I replied that I was more interested in Brigitte Horney than in nuts, but that I seemed to have lost my way. At which point, still holding my hand, she sang the first lines of Hans Fritz Beckmann's theme lyric from *Love, Death and the Devil*, 'So oder ist das Leben', which had made Brigitte Horney very famous.

'Perhaps I've found her,' I said, already humiliated by the awfulness of my attempted joke. 'Such is life.'

'No,' she said, letting go of my hand. 'You've found *me*. Gertrud Schoening. But I am studying film, so I know about this Brigitte.'

How trivial, how pedantic, how dull, how banal.

I writhed to get myself out of the corner I'd backed into.

She picked up the clumsy 'Horney' cue somewhat later, after we'd left the damp, leaf-mouldy autumn woodlands of the botanical gardens and visited Rudi Dutschke's grave at Sankt-Annen, indeed after another visit elsewhere the following day, which was both disappointing and exciting—the 'Horney' thing, that is. It was disappointing because I'd have preferred her to have had the style and intelligence to give me the benefit of the doubt about the leery mistake of 'horny', but exciting because the mushroomy smear on her thigh was exciting, later, when she said, 'And now, as you see, I'm *Horney* after all.'

The early morning light that comes through a dreary internal window into the comfortless little room of the Comfort Hotel on Cuba Street is what I wake to from a performance that's half dream and half memory—half memory because I did approach the dark wood that Gertrud opened between the bare boles of her thighs, but half dream because I'm no longer sure what form my stupidity took. What was its context? Its text? I've had many versions of this waking dream in the seven years since what might best be described as a 'So oder ist das Leben' moment; and despite the unambiguous erection they cause, most of them seem designed to camouflage the circumstances of my humiliation, to rewrite the script, to cast doubt, to encourage ambiguity, to tunnel under truth. Worse, to eschew 'truth' by asking, What kind of truth?—emotional truth, some kind of indeterminate, possibly specious cultural truth that wavered across the mistranslations of our hit-and-miss conversations, or even a truth of fiction as our story unfolded?

Was I in the nut house? Yes, no. No, yes. Ah, but in what sense? What was it about those priceless aromatics, that ancient trade in spicy amelioratives for rotting meat, those corrupting lessons in excess and luxury, that had made me stand as if paralysed among the cinnamons, peppers, nutmegs, cloves and cardamoms?

Did we stroll between the bare trunks of the winter trees, beneath which the rotting deciduous leaves were steaming off a smell of warm mushrooms? Yes, no—but what did I notice then, if we did walk through the botanical gardens: her studious conversation about German films, or the primitive woodland aroma of regeneration?

Did we visit Rudi Dutschke's grave at Sankt-Annen near the university? No, yes. He was my hero when I was doing my Doctorate here at the Free University. He died in 1979, the year I completed the PhD, and he has gone on rebuking every cowardly, self-serving decision I've ever made in my life, and he may even have reduced their potential total over time.

At the graveside, did we try to remember the words of the Wolf Biermann song, 'Drei Kugeln auf Rudi Dutschke'? Yes, no. I doubt it. She didn't know them. I can't remember them now. When I try to, it's the image of his rough boulder headstone that 'comes to mind', whatever that means, with its inscription *Dr. phil. Rudi Dutschke*, and of course its ground cover of simple ivy, how German that is, but no words, and I don't know if the person standing silently beside me is Gertrud or not.

Did those stupid words come out of my mouth? Yes, no.

Not Biermann's, mine. My words.

Yes.

But no.

My phone. It's Peter, texting from Napier. Vero's plane gets in at ten. Meet at 'the house'. I wonder if the quotation marks are his idea.

Yes, no.

But of course yes, because Vero refuses to have a cellphone, god only knows why, it's as if she's still afraid of 'voices', that phase she went through after our mother died.

What was also sexy was the sound of breath refilling Gertrud's chest after one of those long German expostulations—such a vital connection between thinking, speaking and breathing, as if what she was refilling herself with was words, not trivial conversational ones, but ones with the savour and substance of spices and woodlands.

Halyards are rattling in the nasty wind at the Port Nicholson marina, and a smell of warm chlorine gusts from the door of the pool as I go in.

I saw my father and Mick on one of their morning walks just before I went to university up in Auckland, a couple of years before the old man died. I was just leaving Freyberg Pool and they went past at my father's fast clip, elbowing each other, trying for the harbourside track. They didn't see me.

After twenty lengths the mind begins to quieten and a rhythmical consciousness takes over, the muscles stop resisting, the patterns of breath and movement become one, thought moves back into something bodily, like the circulation of blood and oxygen, but also like music. It's Beethoven's Great Fugue in B flat Major, Op. 133 that often works for me, its muscularity, the way it pushes and surges through the thick, deep chords, how it turns and repeats, how it refills itself.

But not if I think about it or want it.

And not today. There they go, the memory lit by clear sunlight as I miss the rhythm of my turn, pushing and shoving, my father's impossible legs performing spindly, nimble moves, Mick's face turned towards him, his mouth open in adoring laughter. God almighty, he was sixteen already.

The venom and disgust in my father's voice. *Why do you want to study Cherman?*

Why do you think.

Why do you want to go to Auckland?

Why do you think.

A man with the welt of a heart-surgery scar the length

of his chest is singing unselfconsciously in the shower, and I want to ask him if he's happy because he's been given a second chance. He grins at me and flicks lather in my direction as if the answer's yes.

I get a banana smoothie from the juice bar at the pool and walk with it along the Parade towards the Point. There's still time before I meet Vero at 'the house'. My hip aches in spite of the swim, or maybe because of it, but there's another ache, it's the one I'd never admit to my father when he was alive, and only to myself after he died, and the one I've spent my adult life denying to Mick, and it's why I don't want to go back along the Parade, and up Cambridge Terrace, and left into Brougham Street, and then around the corner to where the red house will be standing with that choleric complexion stained and aged by the effort of remaining relevant, by the impossible effort of resisting the moment when its self-importance will fall down, when its dignity will collapse, when, like an ageing man falling upon the body of a young woman, the truth of its condition will be naked.

'So, why did you do it?' I said to Gertrud.

'Why not?' was her reply.

What should matter can seem so trivial, and the importance of what seems trivial can pass you by without you noticing that your life has just begun to end.

My second lecture at the Peter Szondi Memorial Symposium in 2007 was intended as a semi-humorous counterpoint to the dour one about Klaus Groth and Johannes Brahms. In it, I rehearsed the spatial performances on 15 August 1961 of Corporal Conrad Schumann and Private Hagen Koch of the East German Army. Schumann became famous for jumping into the West over the initial barbed-wire roll-out of the Wall at the corner of Bernauer Strasse, and Koch for painting the white line that would mark where East Berlin began on the border between Mitte and Kreuzberg. This was my homage to Peter Szondi and his theories about the close performative counterpoint between drama and life, that life is as much about performance as drama is about life. It went down 'quite well' with the audience, who clapped politely and asked some dutifully intelligent questions. There was Gertrud about five rows back, with some young friends, it seemed. She gave me a little wave.

Later in the afternoon we were standing in the Bauhaus Archive looking at the absurd, fetishistic installation of chairs. Breuer's bizarre 1921 'African Chair', and then Neufert, Hartwig, Dieckmann, more and more Breuer of course, Albers, Van Der Rohe, Arndt, Schulze, and on and on, I knew them all, they made me feel sick to my stomach; their skinny, grudging bones were the bones of my father rattling away in all the houses he'd haunted with his uncountable horde of objects designed to repudiate history. These things were zombies—they didn't know how to die, or when to; but I couldn't say any of this to Gertrud, who seemed to be gazing at the chairs with the close, reverend attention of a cultural sychophant.

I, meanwhile, was imagining her bottom filling them.

For that matter, I didn't know why she'd asked to join me, in fact join me again, following the previous day's chance meeting in the nut house, after which we'd parted awkwardly, as if we both acknowledged a discomfort or tension in the maladroit flirtations of our walk in the gardens and to visit Dutschke's grave—she to go home to the flat she no doubt shared with other students, me to attend a stuffy reception at the Norman Foster library building where the symposium was being held.

'My father,' I began, looking at the chairs my father had made his brilliant versions of—me, an ageing professor about to talk about my own father to a nineteen- or twenty-year-old woman young enough to be my, what, *granddaughter*?—but then felt her warm hand slide into mine.

'So,' she said, in that correct tone, 'are you a jumper-over or a drawer of lines, Professor Klepka? A Schumann or a Koch?'

For a moment I can't tell if it's the memory of that moment or the impact of a hand falling heavily on my shoulder that makes my heart stop with a great, ponderous thud, so that when I turn and see Jörg grinning at me I stare at him for a few seconds with my mouth open, waiting for breath—I see his expression freeze around the big smile, expecting recognition, delight, *love* even, so that when I finally get the words out they sound effortful and insincere.

'Jörg! What a surprise!'

He's got running gear on and has the lean, drawn look of someone whose life expectations are outpacing his condition. For some years he used to send me slightly competitive photos or later email attachments of himself taking part in marathons—Around the Bays, in New York, in Chicago, at the top of an immense sand dune somewhere, lying grinning in a starfish shape among people's feet in a paddock while someone turns a hose on him, seeming to get leaner and more stringy with each image until the grin began to look like a rip in the stretched skin of his face. Sometimes he sent links to papers he'd published or lectures he'd given here and there around the world. Sometimes he even appeared in media coverage of political demonstrations, an old leftie. But then the email attachments stopped coming, also the informative Christmas letter, possibly because I stopped reciprocating.

'Not really so surprising,' he says, gripping my hand with both of his, 'since I live here, as you know. But you, Sandy? Why . . . ?'

Why are you here?

Why didn't you recognise me?

Why can't you ever really forgive me?

I can tell by the solicitude of his grip and his by-now forced smile that he knows about my divorce, and he may also have heard on the academic grapevine about my enforced semi-retirement to a .2 single-paper place-holder at the university, with a shared office. He, I've heard on that same grapevine, has retired from Victoria University with full emeritus honours and, since the opportunist rush of academic blood to the head following the Arab Spring, the Occupy movement, Pussy Riot and so forth, a run of requests to guest-lecture about the student movements of the 1960s and '70s, the SDS, the Red Army Faction, urban guerrillas or, alternatively, the revolution of all-conquering love, *und so weiter.* Back when we were both doing PhDs in Dahlem, he was the native departmental darling who diced with political impropriety. He organised campus protests when the RAF activist Holger Meins died after a hunger strike in 1974. He was reprimanded for publishing a paper on state terrorism in which he compared Stammheim

Prison to a Nazi concentration camp. He advocated the assassination of Axel Springer. We both had new young wives with new young babies. He introduced me to Dutschke's work and managed to be both radical and academically successful.

As well as advocating political assassination, he was all for peace and love. He introduced me and Jilly to marijuana, and I can still remember the enthusiastic sounds ('Oh, Jörg!') Jilly made fucking him in the next room while I lay paralysed with stoned vertigo on our bed with his wife, Imogen, who, after a while, just said, matter-of-factly, something like 'Keine grosse Sache', and lit a cigarette. Then one of the babies woke up and began to cry.

I release my hand from Jörg's commiserating clasp and am about to say, 'My brother, Mick, just died,' which is a simple truth, but instead I say, 'We're all going to die one day, Jörg, you can't run away from it,' partly because it just comes out like that, but also because that's what I want to say to him, and also because it's true, it's even truer than the fact of Mick's death. It's a general truth, not a particular one.

And also because, all at once, I'm sick to death of all the bad faith and hypocrisy that's fogging up the view of several simple truths: Jörg's a self-serving fraud, Mick's dead, my career's fucked, my marriage is also fucked, I'm broke, I live in a shitty studio apartment, my son's bankrupted himself again and is about to re-marry with a woman half his age who says she doesn't like his kids, I have trouble getting past twenty pool-lengths into the mind-free zone, I've wanted for years to tell the shit Jörg that I can never forgive him for making Jilly cry out in the next room, let alone for conveniently taking a job in New Zealand, but also . . .

'What's up, Sandy?' says Jörg, stepping back towards the mizzly vista of the grey, ruffled sea, the windswept city, the drab, misty hills. 'Has something happened?'

Has something happened?

And this is the star political phenomenologist of the Freie Universität back in 1979/80? The tame conscience of the de-Nazified faculty? It must be the expression on my face that causes him to re-hear what he's just said, because his face clenches and goes red, as if he's shitting himself.

I think a yelp of laughter comes out of me.

'Sorry, Jörg,' I say. 'Never mind. Good to see you. You'd better keep going, you'll *stiffen up*.' And I turn and begin to walk back towards 'the house', half expecting Jörg to yell after me, 'It's about Jilly, isn't it!'—but of course it's not about Jilly thirty-five years ago, yes, no, but also . . .

He doesn't yell anything at all after me, and has disappeared around the Point when I turn for a quick look. On any other day we could have agreed to meet up to share a bottle of wine and reminisce about this and that, although probably not *that*. We managed it a few times. He'd probably have demanded to know why I didn't tell him I was coming down, I could have stayed with him and whatever his current wife's name is, there's plenty of room, I could have borrowed one of the cars. How are the kids doing, the grandchildren, what are you working on, did I see there was something of yours in *Telos* a few years back, the Peter Szondi memorial issue, you must send me a copy?

But also.

But also because, when I said to Gertrud, 'So why

did you do it?' and she then said, 'Why not?' I then said, 'Because I'm old.'

'Because I'm old, Gertrud. I'm old enough . . .'

'To be my father?' she snapped. 'As if I want to fuck *him*!'

'To be your grandfather!' I snapped back.

'Or him? *Scheisse*!'

I thought she'd go on being angry, or get angrier, but she just laughed.

'So, we talk in clichés now. As if you didn't do this before. I can tell. And anyway, we did it, a few times, it was quite nice, you didn't think about this before?'

I didn't answer, or couldn't think what to say.

'So, it's clear, then,' she said. 'We agree. It doesn't matter.'

This was the last time we 'did it'. The house she shared in Dahlem was full of young people who greeted me politely, brusquely, but without surprise as we went to her room.

'Why does that matter, your age?' She was smoking a cigarette, and blew smoke carefully away from me towards the open window of her bedroom. There was a tree outside, and some long-tailed birds were foraging for something or other among the last few brown leaves. 'I wanted to meet you, I am interested. I liked the way you talk. You worry about being old? About your body? You have quite a nice body, not young, but quite nice.' She gestured at the window with her cigarette. 'It's an autumn body, I also quite like the autumn.'

Quite like.

'Your manner is funny-serious, I like that. I like that you can think. It's quite interesting. So you made me a little bit *horny*. What's the matter with that?'

Little bit.

'Nothing the matter with that.' The words fell out of my mouth like stones. They weren't the ones I wanted to say.

'It's a little bit different. A little bit unusual, an older man. It's quite interesting.'

Little bit. Quite.

'I didn't do that before. So it's different. Maybe that's why . . .'

'Why you get horny,' I said, and heard my grief and shame begin to give the words a hard, nasty sound.

'But it's also because . . .'

I was getting up out of the chair that had her scarf thrown across the back—I could smell her astringent perfume on it, something with citrus, it was the smell of her throat exposed on the pillow when her window was shut, it was what she'd been wearing in the Tropischen Nutzpflanzen.

'And it's also because you are sad.'

I sat down again. 'I'm *sad*?'

'Yes, you are a very sad man.'

'Not *quite* sad.'

'No,' she said, as if what I'd just said was neither a joke nor a taunt. 'I think you are a *very* sad man, and that's why I make an action. Before, I didn't think about doing it. But then the chairs.'

But then the chairs.

This is why I have to get past twenty lengths of the pool, to shut it down, to smother it under the surge of oxygen like Beethoven's great fugue in my blood, my memory of what she said in her chilly room with her cigarette smoke blowing back inside, away from the energetic, resourceful birds in the tree out there in the mid-afternoon dusk, even if I've got it wrong, even if I've rewritten it, even if it didn't happen like that. *But then the chairs.*

'And anyway, Professor Klepka,' she said with a careful smile—that's what she called me, it was a little bit mocking—pushing her cigarette into the ashtray on her desk, where some neat stacks of books and a red and blue striped mug with assorted pens and pencils stood next to a closed laptop and a small vase of wild autumn flowers—I do, I do remember it, all the details—'and anyway, this was just for now, *just for now*, as you know, wasn't it.'

Wasn't it. *Punkt.* Not a question.

Back in the good old days of youthful fervour, Jörg used to quote Dutschke: 'We are not desperate idiots of history.' The sound of stoned Jilly crying out 'Oh, Jörg!' sounded pretty much like a desperate idiot of history to me. And then, in the same place near enough, all those years later, *wasn't it*, the grammar, the tense so precise, an emphatic endorsement of historical closure, and Professor Klepka, another desperate idiot of history, half-running back to his double-glazed accommodation with the scarf he'd stolen from the back of Gertrud's chair, and sitting on the edge of his hotel bed with the scarf's citrus aroma crammed into his mouth to stop the sobs from transmuting into a howl that might have raised the wardens of the nearby Botanischen Garten and sent them hunting among the bare trees with flashlights for some wounded animal, or some creature out of old German myth, but more likely some student prankster the same age as Gertrud Schoening, whose name of course contains the root-word for 'beautiful' in German, and is an old and familiar German name, but whose '-ing' component doesn't really translate, except in the hybrid speech of English and German in which we spoke to each other for three days in 2007, where it can translate perhaps as 'Becoming Beautiful', which Gertrud was, no desperate idiot of history she; no doubt she's long forgotten the moment when she slipped her hand into that of the *quite different* Professor from Auckland, New Zealand, who was made sad, she thought, by the installation of chairs in the Bauhaus-Archiv Museum für Gestaltung, Klingelhöfferstrasse 14, Tiergarten, 10785 Berlin, but she didn't know why.

Because that was when he'd remembered, or realised, why he'd come to Berlin in the first place, all those years ago in 1974.

Why do you want to go to Germany?

Why do you think.

My father's terrible anger. My father's terrible shame.

Only she didn't know anything about that, and I never told her.

My father's face had been crimson with fury back then, or that's how I read it, but lately I've begun to wonder if it wasn't grief and frustration. His mad desire not to be a desperate idiot of history, and now look what this stupid son of his is doing.

I've still got the banana smoothie in one hand but it tastes like sickly gluey shit, so I chuck it with unnecessary force into a rubbish bin on the corner of Courtenay Place by Downstage Theatre. This used to be Micky's zone; whatever strife he got into during his time at high school, and he got into plenty, it mostly happened around here. I've got just over twenty minutes before Vero's going to turn up at 'the house', but I take a detour down as far as Taranaki Street and then back up the other side of Courtenay Place past the strip joint and the TAB. There's a bunch of panhandlers there, including a crazy-eyed man with long hair wearing a sleeveless puffer jacket with synthetic stuffing sprouting out of it, who's raving about burning Bibles or something. How easy it would have been for Mick to end up like that, although perhaps he did in a sense, only he had a four-bedroom Mount Vic house all to himself, the crazy bastard. He just couldn't let it go. Couldn't or wouldn't, I don't know which.

But it's indeed true that Professor Klepka's *very sad*, so I stop halfway down the next block, and turn around, and go back across the Tory Street intersection with a drab crowd of pedestrians to the TAB, because that's where Mick rang from, so he said, the last time I heard from him. A few punters are standing outside on the footpath, smoking, and there seems to be a cartoon-cut-out Mick shape among them, a silhouette, a poor ghost.

And a very good morning to you, too, Sandy.

His harsh voice ranting down the phone yesterday about some horse and an arts page reporter—I've got no idea what was going on in that amazing mind of his. The moment you tried to put the word 'help' next to the word 'Sandy', some kind of violence would result. But this was different. This felt different. Though we'd always fought, I knew my crazy brother.

I'd walked around Victoria Park after leaving the gym and Mick's phone call—an acid of unease was agitating all my joints and I needed to walk it off. The great piles of brown plane-tree leaves were wet after a night's downpour, but a Japanese woman photographer was lying on her stomach in the middle of a heap of them, aiming the extended snout of a video camera at a man in an orange visibility jacket and knee-length lycra running pants who was sprinting flat out towards her along the edge of the trees' shadow line—flitting through the bright dappled sunlight, then stopping with a great huff of breath just short of the videoist and trudging back to his starting place. They kept it up the whole time as I walked around the park, which was full of sunlight and the cheerful, busy sound of traffic on the motorway overpass, and the yapping of dogs chasing balls and sticks, and the hearty shrieks of a personal trainer urging her small group of young women to *work it, work it*!—and the lovelier it all was, with those big melodramatic Auckland clouds in the blue sky, and the autumn smell of damp grass, and the more I saw the *aliveness* of everything, including the orange-vested sprinter, the heavier the sense of dread and grief in my chest became, and the more the gravelly sound of Mick's voice replayed in my head. I don't hate my brother, but I can't stand him, and his behaviour over the house is stupid and selfish—but every so often, when he goes off the rails, I see that Clyde Quay Primary kid with the top button of his shirt done up, or the grinning Kraftwerk crazy in his stupid vinyl jacket, or I rehear those stories he made up.

How many times had this happened—he'd got some paranoid idea and then gone on a bender of some kind, usually involving those fucking drugs, or done something crazy like getting the back lawn at the house concreted over, and all any of us could do was say to ourselves, Don't try to put 'help' and 'Mick' together?

But this felt different. By the time I'd walked around the park it was getting late, so I caught the Link bus up the hill to the university instead of walking, and the horrible dread sat down with me in a seat towards the back. From there I could see the length of the bus, and I watched a young woman near the front begin to comb and tidy her dark hair into a kind of bun, her quick methodical fingers flicking and tucking, while another young dark-haired woman next to her began to notice what she was doing—her head kept turning to take quick peeks at the hair-work going on next to her. Then the first one noticed herself being noticed, and offered the comb to the woman next to her in the seat. I saw a fragment of her friendly smile in profile, the bright glint of teeth. Perhaps they were friends? Then the second woman accepted the comb, and quickly and neatly reorganised her own hair with little shakes of her head. Then she gave the comb back. Another teeth-glint. They were like a couple of birds on a branch in the sunshine at the park, grooming together in the fresh, flickering light. Then another, older woman sitting behind the two young groomers on the other side of the bus noticed what they were doing and began to push her own straight, blond hair back behind her ears. And then a man with a huge pile of dreads under his big knitted cap couldn't stop himself from adjusting the load of hair on his head, putting both hands up to fix his coloured hat. And then a shaved-head gym guy put first one hand and then the other up to the smooth crown of his head, and gave it a bit of a shine.

I got off the bus a stop earlier than I'd planned, because the outbreak of grooming was like a message about Mick's loneliness, as if he'd been hoping that his phone call to me would set off a chain reaction of some kind that would unite us, but of course I didn't know that any more than I knew what had set him off on his own. But I couldn't help it. All at once it was unbearable to stay on the bus with the sound of my voice saying, 'Shut the fuck up, Mick, and stop wasting my time.'

The last thing I ever said to him.

Inside the TAB under the bleak neon light there's a desultory bustle of activity, but no one seems to be talking to anyone else much. The payphones are on the far side of the room. I pick one up and listen to the waiting hum that comes from it. The mouthpiece smells of cigarettes.

I take the short-cut up Tory Street and stop around the corner to blow my nose and wipe up the tears. Very sad Professor Klepka. A merry babble of voices and the sound of clattering plates and cups come from Caffe l'Affare, and a jostling bunch of people going in give me quick looks over their shoulders. It's late already, but Vero won't be, and she won't know where the key is.

Only the nominated 'next of kin' knows that.

I cross the busy Cambridge Terrace intersection by the smelly pub I know Mick liked to frequent—the twin-carriageway vista of my childhood and youth has barely changed, and nor has the grainy filtration of the light on a day like this, with that low metallic cloud greying the air and taking the shine off the wet pavements, and, it seems to me as it used to when I lived here, infusing the movement of traffic up towards the Mount Victoria tunnel, and the heads-down scuttle of pedestrians, with a kind of dull menace, as if history was indeed something not even my—our—hyper-optimistic father could naysay.

People used to apply the epithet 'grungy' to this aspect of the city, as if it was a virtue to be celebrated, but towards the end of my time here, and not least from the moment when my father's scorn turned nasty over my decision to leave and go to Auckland, let alone to study German, the word 'grungy' began to stand for everything I hated about the place, and have gone on hating ever since, not least its self-congratulating, provincial, solipsistic gloating over its vaunted 'grunginess'.

Yesterday as I walked from the bus stop up the hill through Albert Park to the university, trying but failing to get rid of the sound of my own voice saying 'Shut the fuck up, Mick, and stop wasting my time', I encountered the happy family groups who were gathering in graduation photo-opportunity clusters with big bouquets of flowers, and the autumn flowerbeds in their glory, and the fountain, and the coloured silks of the graduation robes, and the differently thrilled and proud intonations of different languages, and I might as well have said aloud, in fact I probably did, *How do we open up to these bright glimpses of another world than ours?*

What did I mean, 'wasting my time'?

What does it mean, 'desperate idiots of history'?

Agnes and Vero came up from Wellington for my graduation. We stood together in this park. Vero was chatting about the Japanese anemones in the herbaceous borders and Agnes was pleased by the fountain.

By the foodcourt in the student union yesterday morning a sound stage had been set up, and a group of big enthusiastic fa'afafine were belting out or maybe lip-synching show-biz standards with a ragged brass section in behind. Someone grabbed my arm—it was one of my students, not one of the brightest, but all lit up with her graduation moment.

'Thanks for everything,' she said, and gave me a shy, chaste kiss on the cheek.

I didn't remember her name.

Vero is standing by the shuttered garage when I come up the hill towards the house. We seem to be lining each other up as we move steadily into focus. She's ignoring a plump ginger cat that's rubbing its arched body against her shins. Did Mick have one? That seems improbable. Though she's my sister, Vero's kiss seems on the face of it even less intimate than that of the student yesterday, the one whose name I don't remember.

Vero and I hang on to each other for a while as if waiting like boxers to see who will break the hold first. I think what I'm saying into the springy mass of her hair is, *How do we open up to these bright glimpses of another world than ours?*—but that's just what's running through my mind.

'You're looking sprightly,' is what I say, and she breaks our hold and pushes me away. There's a look of forthright annoyance on her face. She gives my arms a little shake.

'Jesus, I hate that word,' she says.

'What about *in good shape*?'

'We don't have to do this, Sandy,' she says, and before I can say, 'Do what?' she pulls me back into the embrace and blurts, 'Poor old Micky,' into my chest. It's true that she's in good shape; her body against me is firm and steady, and her sobs are honest and powerful. Then, in that no-nonsense way she's always had, she pulls free again, gets a tissue from the pocket of her parka and blows her nose loudly, never once taking her eyes off me.

I don't really know what she's looking at, or for—maybe she wants to see some sign of my sadness, the sadness of Professor Klepka, but that seems to belong somewhere else now.

'So, have you been in yet?' says my blunt sister, whose speech always sounds like an abbreviation of some more comprehensive thought. It *sounds* no-nonsense, but has the complicating effect of making you hesitate before answering, so that usually, as now, she just moves on impatiently. 'No? So, okay, let's get cracking, where's the key?'

The key's in the front pouch of my swimming-gear backpack, and a look of confusion and annoyance makes Vero's face flinch as I unzip the pouch and get the keys out. There are several, on a keyring, for the garage, the front door and the door to the studio at the back.

'Didn't know you had those,' says Vero, but then she just turns and walks up the path, trundling her small suitcase.

I have the keys for the same reason I have the Trust documents with the lawyer's note explaining that the will Agnes made has codicils to be opened when the house is finally disposed of—all of which Vero also has, being a trustee, but not the keys, there was only one set provided. Not counting Mick's one.

It's the 'little things'.

The path is very clean and swept, the overhanging branches of the old taupata neatly trimmed back. The concrete apron above the garage has also been swept free of moss and leaves, but the reddish street-side wall of the house is even blotchier and more faded than the last time I saw it. When Vero turns around suddenly with a look of annoyance and grief on her face, it too is blotchy and red.

'Go on, then,' she says.

Inside, the house doesn't smell musty or dirty, and I don't know why I expected it to, since Mick was always compulsively fastidious. There are heavy wooden blinds on the windows in the big front downstairs rooms, but even in the dim light it's clear they are completely empty. There's plenty of light in the large open-plan back room with its French doors opening out to where the lawn was until Mick got it concreted over. There's a big plasma TV with a horrible padded La-Z-Boy armchair in front of it, and against the southern wall a neatly made single bed, the pale sheet folded precisely over the duvet, whose geometrical cover pattern I recognise. The large kitchen benches are bare. My father's pride-and-joy floor-to-ceiling bookshelves are empty except for five rows of tightly packed DVDs—there must be hundreds of them. There's a fresh smell of household cleaner, something lemony. That's all there is.

'Oh, Micky,' says Vero, but she's not crying anymore—she stands flat on her feet with her legs planted somewhat apart, as if preparing to make some large physical effort, of lifting or reorganising, but there's nothing to reorganise. The austere dimensions of Mick's life are daunting; it's as though he's deliberately edited the traces of his day-to-day routines so as to pre-empt any interpretation of them.

I imagine we're both visualising Mick sitting in his La-Z-Boy in front of the lifeless TV screen—I am; how could Vero not be?

'Do you want to have a look at the rest?' I say. 'I mean,

the rest of the house?'

'I could do with a cup of tea first,' says Vero, and starts opening cupboards in the kitchen. They're all empty, except for a shelf of household cleaners. 'There isn't even a hot water jug,' shouts my sister, and begins to laugh. Then she opens the outsize fridge. There must be at least three dozen bottles of beer lined up neatly on the racks. 'What the hell,' she says. 'Want one?'

I don't say anything, but she gets a couple out and opens them with the bench-top device my father built in to the thick kauri plank with its worn, bevelled edge. The bottle-opener was one of his jokes, a little homage to the vernacular, and he loved it—he used to make the caps of the big brown bottles fly across the room.

'Cheers, Micky,' says Vero. She takes a sip from her bottle and grimaces, and is about to take another, but stops with the bottle tilted against her lips when I say, 'Martin really loved the mad bugger, didn't he.'

I feel the word 'Martin' hesitate in the moment before I say it, as if it has to jump over something.

I don't want my beer, and I put the bottle on the bench that's between my sister and me. She lowers her drink and is looking at me as though she's been expecting something like this, but like what? All I mean is, it's no surprise that Mick ended up in the house; it was always his as far as our father was concerned. But that's not something you can see until you're in it with him gone. All its details, like the bench-top bottle-opener, and the minimal bevel on the edges of the bench top, and the beautifully proportioned rectangular bookshelves, and how they are a horizontal match for the vertical dimensions of the tall window beside them—even the perversity of the La-Z-Boy—all seem to be framing and annotating the love those two had, according to which Mick could do no wrong. And now that he's gone, the love has emptied from the room into which he'd compressed its last, concentrated trace. So now it just feels empty.

We must have left the front door ajar, because the cat from the street wanders in with its tail erect and runs away from Vero when she tries to chase it back out. She pulls the bolts on the French doors and pushes them open in their brass track, kicking a rolled-up towel out of the way, and the cat escapes into the concrete yard and then sits, not looking back, licking at its shoulder.

Lit from behind by the grey, metallic light, my stocky sister still looks like the kid who might have stood just there with her back to the lawn where our father was subjecting the natural world to his system of rectangles and stripes, meanwhile acting the goat for Mick's benefit, or later for the cleaner's weird kid, whose thrilled shrieks used to make Vero put her hands over her ears and come inside through the French doors, screwing her face up.

She's screwing her face up now, ostensibly because she doesn't like the taste of the beer but also to make the shape of her question.

'Why do you think that was?'

'Why do I think what was?' I know what she's asking, but I want her to say it and without making a face.

'You know—why did Martin love Micky? I mean, so much?'

'Why did Agnes love you?' I say.

'Here we go again,' says Vero, and begins to laugh.

'Jesus Christ, Sandy, just listen to us. Here we are, a couple of grandparents—actually in my case about to be a great-grandparent, probably—and we're still doing the favourites thing.'

But that isn't what I mean.

Now, after all this time, and after the lives we've lived away from the house, and away from its framing devices and memory-opening gadgets, and now that its last concentrated dreg of life has been emptied out of it, the question of why Martin and Agnes loved any of us seems to have moved out of range of answers, like the cat with its casual disregard for what's just happened—and now it suddenly bolts out of sight around the corner, and I hear its claws ripping an excited ascent of the trunk of the elder whose delicate blossom Agnes used to make into a fragrant, volatile 'champagne', and which my father used to greet mockingly by lifting his baseball cap when its first clusters of white cloudy flowers appeared—some kind of Cherman tradition. Sometimes, when Agnes used to open one of the elder champagnes out on the deck, her scream and the explosion were all that was left of it—the contents vaporising across the orderly nap of the lawn, just a finger's depth left humming in the bottom of the bottle.

Used to.

The pressure of all that bottled-up time.

'We'd better get over to the hospital,' I say. There's a kind of high-pressure zone between my sister and me, and it's pushing everything we need to say to each other out to the margins of what's happening.

'You mean, identify Mick?' That practical, no-nonsense manner again.

'Some time before twelve,' I say, but really it's before he too just disappears entirely, the way time has from the inside of the house—the way the house's purpose as a container has, all at once, become redundant. 'Then we have to see the lawyer,' I say.

Vero is looking around the almost empty room. 'We'll have to come back,' she says. 'I'll leave my bag.'

She takes our bottles of beer to the sink and tips them out. There's a washed glass and several empties next to the sink. Mick was drinking by himself, but somebody's tidied up. I see my shrewd sister take note of this, and pause, but she doesn't say anything.

As we're getting into the taxi, though, she does come out with one of those blunt, coded remarks.

'Know what this feels like?' she says. 'It's as though Mick was the plug, and now that he's gone . . .'

'Been pulled,' I say.

'. . . it's as though everything's just drained away.'

'Down the gurgler.'

'Down the bloody gurgler,' says Vero, with a kind of relish. 'What do you reckon?'

'Same,' I say, hearing us slip into the speech of our childhood.

A little way along Brougham Street there's a minor traffic jam where some of the day patients at the halfway house are being dropped off.

'Christ,' says Vero. 'Imagine having to deal with one of them on a daily basis.'

I'm tempted to point out that Mick pretty much was one but that neither of us knows who did. It wasn't us, anyway.

'Remember Sampan?' she says.

I'd have said I didn't, but I do now, watching the variously disarticulated people struggle into or out of their backpacks. 'I wonder what happened to them?' I say, but in fact I don't wonder, and nor does Vero, apparently, because she doesn't pursue the matter—though she's looking out the window at the little jostling crowd, and I can tell she's thinking about something, but whatever it is she's not sharing.

The taxi driver's a middle-aged or older Indian or Bangladeshi man with nicely groomed hair. His cab is fresh, with a smell of recent upholstery cleaner, something a bit sweet and flowery. There are real flowers, some miniature pinkish chrysanthemums, in a small long-necked vase attached to the dashboard by a clever home-made bracket. The sleeves of his shirt have crisply ironed creases. He's driving with a kind of languid pleasure, as if there's no hurry to get to the next fare, and sneaking looks at us in his rear-view mirror. As we wait more patiently than usual for a gap in the traffic by the Basin Reserve, he half-turns to us and says, over his shoulder, 'That's your house?'

Neither Vero nor I answers. We look at each other—her face has a blank expression that I imagine mirrors mine. Probably the driver takes us for a couple.

'Sorry,' he says, 'don't mean to be rude. But it's interesting.'

'What is?' says Vero in her abrupt way.

'Your house,' says the driver, making that assumption. 'It's very modern, isn't it? Up-to-date.'

'Actually, it was built in 1947,' I say. 'By an architect called Martin Klepka.'

Vero gives me an 'Oh, please' look and mouths 'actually'.

'He's probably well known?' says the driver, as if apologising.

'Not anymore,' I say.

'But still nice place to live in?'

I sense the man's giving up hope, so I say, 'It's been a wonderful house to live in,' hearing how my carefully provisional grammar winds itself around the truth.

'Yes, wonderful,' Vero says, and when I look at her she's grinning, and her eyes are shining with mirth or tears, I can't tell which.

'You know,' says the driver, emboldened by the good news, 'you got to have a house you can be happy in. Otherwise.'

We both wait for whatever doom is going to follow 'otherwise', but nothing's forthcoming.

'Otherwise you can't be happy?' offers Vero, as if the tautology needs to be bolted together.

'Exactly!' says the driver. 'I got all my kids houses,' he adds in an offhand way.

I'm daring Vero to say, 'And they're all happy?' But she just murmurs, 'Good for you, my friend.' And then, 'So I guess you'll be driving taxis for a few more years yet?'

The driver laughs. 'Nah,' he says. 'Part time now. Pocket money. They got to look after themselves. Pay the mortgage, all that. Be looking after *us* soon enough, won't they.'

'Lucky for you,' says Vero. 'Can't see that happening with our lot.' She winks at me. 'Too busy ruining their own lives to worry about ours.' She clears her throat in a self-admonishing, apologetic kind of way, and then, as if she's been holding it in, lets go with an extended rattle of laughter, throwing her head back and slapping her thigh.

'Excuse me,' she says, wiping her eyes. 'But, you know, happy in spite of that, the silly buggers. Wouldn't you say, Sandy?'

'Last I heard, Joe'd just bankrupted himself again, this time on a super-yacht contract for some Russian oligarch, and was leaving Mandy for a young woman he'd met at the Boat Show.'

'And my seventeen-year-old granddaughter's pregnant,' shouts Vero, beginning to laugh again, and I can't help myself, the laughter comes out in a great efflorescent fountain, like the elder champagne from one of Agnes's explosive bottles, and Vero and I fall together and hang on to each other, her face has gone all blotchy again, and the snot starts to run out of my nose.

'Here,' says Vero, pushing a tissue against my face, 'clean yourself up, you fool.'

The taxi driver's shoulders are shaking. 'My son,' he says, and pauses. 'Excuse me.'

'No, go on, please, don't mind us,' says Vero, who's calming down.

'Very rebellious boy, too clever also. He's in love with this girl, going to marry her, doesn't matter what we say, we are old-fashioned monsters. But then he goes to visit his cousins back over in Puri, seaside holiday and all that, and boom! Arranged marriage, old school.'

'And they're happy?' says Vero. 'It worked out, contra-romance-wise?'

'No way!' says the driver, laughing heartily now. 'She just left him! Said he's too serious!'

He toots his horn as we go up the steps to the hospital.

'Goodness me,' says my sister. 'That was refreshing.' She's holding my arm, and all at once we both seem to notice this. 'We're okay, aren't we?' she says, stopping in front of the main entrance. 'I mean, you and me?' She reaches up and pats my cheek. 'Too serious, Sandy. I mean, one can be, can't one?'

'One can,' I say. Our old teasing game.

But then I just have to.

'Why didn't you respond to my emails, Vero? What took you so long? The voice-messages?'

The relief and lightness don't drain from her face, as I expected they would, regretting what I'd just said the moment I said it. She pats my face again.

'Come off it, Sandy,' she says. 'What are you claiming now—intuition? Mick just conked out. You didn't know he would. Give yourself a break.'

'The last thing I said to him, on the phone, was, Stop wasting my time, or something shitty like that.'

'And *now* you feel bad?' Suddenly, my sister's face has her particularly intense expression of scorn on it. 'So this is about *you*? Or you think saying that killed him?'

'No,' I say. 'Not about me. And of course I didn't kill him. But yes, I do feel bad.'

'Fuck's sake,' says Vero. 'You can't have it both ways. Make up your mind. Do you feel responsible, or did Mick just die?'

'He just died,' I say lamely, knowing I've surrendered something but I'm not sure what.

'Okay, then,' says Vero, 'let's do whatever's required, shall we?'

I've seen dead people before—Martin and Agnes, of course, and a few friends and colleagues, and a few lying on marae. My father wasn't my father by the time I saw him. I came down from Auckland and encountered this serene lookalike, with lipstick on his calm mouth and a sheen of clammy stillness on his high unwrinkled forehead, whose repose in my father's case would have been the prelude to some prank or other, something inappropriate and wicked, so that I waited for a while for him to rise up out of the coffin at the undertakers and produce some kind of mocking effect, the sound of a toy trumpet, or a great fart, or a 'Boo!'—but he didn't. Agnes was different. She died twenty years after him. She was still alive when I came down from Auckland, but she'd gone past recognising anyone, although she said 'Hello' when I finally got there, but it should have been 'Goodbye,' and there's no way she could have known who I was. There was almost nothing left of her, just a little bundle of sticks, and when she'd gone and the nurse asked Mick and me if we wanted to help clean her, I said no, because what was left there on the hospital bed wasn't my mother anymore, and I didn't want to look at what she *wasn't*. But I saw the look Mick gave me, which was pretty much what it had always been, something like *You coward dick-head fucking wanker.*

I've never quite believed the toe-tag thing—it seems like a cliché out of crime fiction—but there it is, on Mick's toe.

And it is Mick, all right, at the other end of the silly thing on his toe, only how can I say it? He looks great, his face not exactly calm, more a little smug and ironic, as if he's had the last laugh, a bit weathered but handsome despite needing a shave, his long grey hair pushed back off that high forehead, the big eyes closed. It is Micky the way I'd hoped he could be when he was alive, and the way I knew he was for that matter, the most unusual of us three, the brightest without doubt, but . . .

My inventory is veering off towards 'but most fucked up', but the brother who's half-smiling and asleep in front of me doesn't look in the least fucked up. He looks as though he's had a beer and called it a day. Knowing that he's had some kind of last laugh or other.

But none of us can know that.

There's a strange dry smell in the mortuary, though in effect everything in it seems to have been made out of a liquid substance, like viscous time, a metallic or porcelain emulsion of memory that has, just briefly, ceased to flow. Has desiccated itself irrespective of its conditions or contexts, and has just stopped, at once dry and frozen, at once motionless and about to be gone.

We sign the papers and agree to nominate a funeral director, and then walk together on what feels like a strangely veering, nauseating conveyor belt towards the hospital exit. Outside, the air is cool and damp, and Vero's face, too, has a moist, chilly sheen on it, as if the surging emotional colours of the past couple of hours have drained away.

'Well, that was him all right,' she says. 'That was our Micky.' She's studying my face—her eyes moving around and across it.

'What?' I say.

'How do you feel?' she says. And then, in that can't-wait way of hers, 'Who should we tell? Do we know who his friends were?'

'I feel like having some lunch,' I say, 'if you want to know the truth. I want to sit down and eat something good, and have a nice bottle of wine and raise a glass to Mick, and not worry about the next bit.'

I can't believe I've said that, but I'm glad I did. It's as though some kind of propriety, a sanguinity, has begun to give the day its appropriate shape.

Vero takes my arm again, only this time she hugs it close to her body.

'The lamb rack with Nepalese spiced cheek at Logan Brown,' she says. 'Or the bistro monkfish, if you're being careful.' Of course she knows this stuff. It's what she and Peter do.

We're quite early, but the maître d' knows Vero.

'Veronica!' he cries. 'What brings you to town?'

'I'm catching up with my brother,' she says.

We lift the first glass and look each other in the eye, and clink, but neither of us says the words.

'In case you're wondering,' says Vero, giving her glass a waggle, 'I'm doing okay. I'm allowed two. Watch me.' Then she pauses. 'Can't say the same for Pete, unfortunately. Permanent loop in the tracks, there.' Her eyes are scanning across my face again. I know what's coming. 'You?'

'What about me?'

'Come off it, Sandy. How often do we get to do this?'

I'm having the lentil and ricotta cake bistro entrée—it's tasty but a bit sticky, so you can't talk around it. I finish my mouthful and take a good swallow of wine. Those whose company accounts can afford the business lunch at Logan Brown are beginning to barge boastfully into the restaurant. I find myself measuring my reply to Vero's understated interrogation—of my private life, health and happiness, professional situation, and more than likely sexual status near the top of her interests—against the space between the noisy bonhomie of the business lunchers and the silence in the mortuary where my brother Michael Klepka seemed content to keep his mouth shut.

'Good,' I say.

My sister's regarding me steadily, and I can't tell whether she's going to smile next, or get annoyed—whether she's going to say something affectionately mocking like, *Oh, Sandy, stop being so mysterious!* or peevish, like, *Oh, Sandy, lighten up for the love of god!* But she just waits, and somewhere between the blather of the expense-account crowd and the stillness in my brother's expression I find my cue. I'm not really telling Vero anything she doesn't know already, but at least now she's hearing it from me. Coming on eight years ago I met a young German woman who broke my heart through no fault of her own, I lost the plot, Jilly divorced me and bought me out of our house, I gave the house money to Joe to save his boat-building business but he lost the lot, I couldn't handle my work anymore and got a performance-review soft-sacking, these days I travel free on the bus with a superannuant card, my main extravagance is the gym because I don't want to be old, and it's been quite a while since I ate in a good restaurant.

I raise my glass to her. 'But, *Dum vivimus, vivamus*!' Her eyebrows go up. 'While we live, let us live!'

She covers her glass with one hand when I go to top it up. I refill my own. Not much sleep last night, or the one before for that matter, and my third glass of wine has begun to make my cheeks feel numb, as if I've got a grin fixed on my face.

'So,' says Vero, with a mocking waggle of her head, 'no more hanky-panky, eh?'

'Not even one glass, so to speak,' I say.

'Now *that* I find hard to believe, you sexy beast.' She's tucking into her lamb-rack main, and is talking with one cheek full, like a busy squirrel or something. Then she puts her knife and fork down with a clatter. 'I've never told you this, or anyone else for that matter,' she says. Then she picks the fork up again, and refills her cheek, as if what she's about to tell me can only be uttered with a full mouth—as if the message needs to be stoked up.

'What?' I've got the small bistro serving of monkfish in front of me but I can't get started with it. The appetite I thought I had seems to be waiting for something to trigger it again—a desire, a lust, a curiosity.

'I had an affair in Venice that time I went with Sophie,' says Vero, looking me in the eye. Her throat gulps as though swallowing something whole.

'When Agnes died? Then?' My sister's eyes have begun to shine and blink; she's nodding her head, and one hand is clenching and unclenching around her napkin on the table. A tipsy surge of pity and love propels my hand across the table to grab hers. 'Oh, Vero, that must have been awful,' I say.

'No,' she says, and two identical tears run down into her grin. 'It was great. It had nothing to do with Agnes, or anyone else. What was it you said, *Dum* something?'

'*Dum vivimus, vivamus.*'

'Bugger it, pour me another, Sandy.' She wipes her eyes on the napkin and takes a decent swallow. 'Just keep an eye on me, will you, brother? I need to get home in one piece. Things are a bit ropey back at the ranch.'

Mick was always aggressive and usually derisive on the battered subject of culture versus biology—for him the human world was basically no different from the world of bacteria, except that we'd deluded ourselves into believing that consciousness trumped neurotransmitters and biochemistry. But the appetite with which I now begin to enjoy the monkfish on my plate, even though it's getting cold, is certainly because of the surge of affection I feel for my sister when she begins to tell me her story about the German man who'd smoked a cigar in bed after making love to her—or rather, the way she tells it, with the enthusiasm of someone who hasn't had the chance to talk about this before, or hasn't wanted to—who'd smoked a cigar in bed after they'd fucked each other to a standstill. Quite possibly, after she'd fucked him to a standstill. It's the pleasure of our intimacy and the joy of a good story that makes me hungry again, as well as the prurient interest being taken in my sister's unabashed account by some of the neighbouring diners. She does a good impersonation of a large German male blowing smoke at the ceiling.

'Did you ever see him again?' I ask.

'Only in my dreams,' she says, sitting back with a self-satisfied smirk. 'Because then you phoned, remember?' Her eyes have the slightly awash look of someone whose tolerance for drink is out of proportion to their desire to talk and therefore to their need to keep their hand on the tiller of narrative. 'Otherwise, who knows?'

'I can tell you one thing for free,' I say, seeing a need to slow her down.

'What's that?' She pours herself the last glass in the bottle and looks at me. 'Sorry,' she says. 'Shall we get another?'

'You were a mess when you got back.'

'Nothing to do with Uli,' she says. 'Ul-richhh. Christ, was your German wench that much fun?'

'What about a sticky with dessert,' I say as Vero begins to look for the waiter.

She heaves a sigh. 'Okay,' she says, 'but answer the question.'

'Was my German wench that much fun?'

'Sorry, Sandy,' she says. 'Insensitive of me.'

'She was a lovely girl,' I say. 'But overall it was mostly just sad.'

The roar of the lunching crowd has begun to get bolder, as if to compete with the unnecessary piped music, which is a jazz trio, Bill Evans by the sound of it, and I'm beginning to have trouble hearing what Vero's saying. She's going on about our mother, Agnes, how she always seemed to live between the words that describe where and how we are: now and then, here and there, angry and amused, sad and happy. But then I hear her repeat something, a bit loudly.

'But you were always sad, Sandy. You were the sad one, I was the bad one and Micky was the mad one. Remember?'

Vero's having a late-harvest Riesling with her crème brûlée and I've got a grappa with my coffee. I down both quickly and head for the toilet. Sad, bad and mad. Or rather, when I shuffle them into the right order, sad, mad and bad.

I pay the bill on the way back to our table.

It's a short walk down to the lawyer's on Blair Street off Courtenay Place. We're halfway along Cuba Street before Vero comes out with it.

'Do you think he fucked us all up?'

I know she means our father, not poor old Mick, whose harm was mostly confined to what he did to himself.

The usual 'grungy' types are hanging about along the mall; there's a fairly lagered-up crowd outside the Irish pub, they're eating steaks with chips and punching at each other; there's a lone busker playing wheedly Paul Simon songs behind an empty hat on the footpath, and a few deadshits inhaling from plastic bags under their coats. A little kid has just fallen into the bucket fountain and is yelling blue murder. A bit further back the way we've come some people with plenty of money have been eating expensive lunches. What's liberating is not feeling the need to make sense of any of it.

It's been a while.

'Of course he did. The bastard totally fucked us.'

She takes my arm again. 'Luck-y,' she says. 'Luck-y for us. All the better for it.'

I don't know what she means by that. 'And Mick?' I say. 'What about Mick? I mean, really?' I make her stop and look at me. *Sad and bad*, the survivors.

Her eyes are slightly glassy with wine and optimism. 'Mick was Mick,' she says. 'He could be a nasty bugger. He thought you were an idiot. He thought I was boring. But he was fucked. He was the most fucked. And now he's dead.' Despite the winey swagger in her expression, her gaze doesn't waver, and she grips my arms tightly and makes me look at her. 'So it doesn't matter anymore. There's nothing you can do about it.' She gives me a little shake. 'He's not going to be ringing you up again, Sandy, and having a go.'

The law firm's offices are up one flight of stairs in a refurbished warehouse where the old fruit and vegetable markets used to be. I had a school-holiday job there once, pushing barrows for the energetic, bullying Chinese buyers. They used to overload me and then yell if stuff fell off. Our father made us get holiday jobs, but when Mick refused he let him work in the furniture studio off Adelaide Road. When Sad and Bad complained that this was unfair, the old bastard just said that life wasn't fair either. He wasn't wrong about that.

Some of the original market brickwork has been left exposed in the law offices; there are skylights in the roof, and the floor is broad, sanded-back rimu planks. There was a craze for this kind of nonsense a few years ago, but short-lived, so that now the place looks like a carefully preserved specimen, a museum of itself and at the same time a palimpsest with its plain mercantile past showing through a veneer of quickly dated taste. It's the kind of thing that used to make my father laugh—the provincial colonialist obsession with heritage, a kind of historical bad faith. I don't remind Vero of this, though I want to, just to wind her up.

The young woman who comes into the meeting room with our Trust folder and holds out her hand for us to shake looks like an intruder in this space of nostalgia—Thai-boxing fit, short-cropped hair, an earlobe full of rings, black cotton sweatshirt and pants.

'Sorry about your brother Michael,' she says, pouring us all glasses of water. She's not, of course, but she's got what Jilly calls good lawyer's manners. Jilly's got them too, among the best, QC sharp; they work by uttering emotion at the same time as sealing it off from engagement, so that sincerity is mostly a form of rebuff.

'I'm sorry for the short notice,' I can't resist saying, not liking her much, but then a little smile breaks through her sophomore cool. Of course I could hardly have contacted her any sooner, is what it says.

'It's okay,' she says. 'I've had time to look at the documents and get the investment statements.'

We go through the familiar Trust paperwork. We've all had yearly drawing rights—up to ninety per cent of our shares of the invested capital. Jilly and I spent mine years ago, building the house she still lives in, when we were a professor–lawyer combination and often ate at good restaurants. Half my percentage of the house settlement will be hers under the terms of our separation, and she'll take it too. What's left plus a smidgen of capital might buy me some time at the gym. Mick's draw-down share has also 'maxed-out', says the lawyer, but his residual capital share and its income will now become part of the consolidated investment fund, of which the majority belongs to Vero, who's never touched a cent since Agnes died twenty-six years ago. The lawyer, whose name is Sue, is wearing thin black-rimmed glasses to read, and she looks at Vero over the top of them in a rehearsed kind of way.

'It's an unusual arrangement,' she says, meaning, I suppose, likely to generate conflict.

Vero doesn't respond to this—perhaps Sue expects her to be surprised and thrilled by her situation, in which case she doesn't know my shrewd sister, who takes a good long drink of water and then says, in as many words, thanks for wasting my time, now can we get to the sealed codicil that

Agnes left, please?

Neither of us has mentioned this to each other—me because I'd forgotten about it, or if not exactly forgotten, stopped thinking about it after Jilly and I had finished filling our lawyer-professor house with Provençal terrines and a bespoke rolling-ladder library bookshelf wall in recycled kauri.

The way Vero's looking not at me but at the lawyer, her eyes fully alert despite their winey shine, suggests she's been avoiding the subject of the codicil.

Sue has a nice thin designer paper knife, and she slits the sealed envelope that Agnes had instructed be opened by the trustees when the house that Martin Klepka built in 1947 is finally vacated by all of them. She takes out a single folded sheet of paper and pushes it across the table towards us.

'This is to be read by you, the surviving trustees, in the presence of a lawyer, which I guess is me,' she says, with another carefully rueful smile.

It's now that Vero looks at me. She rests her hand on the folded sheet.

'Sampan,' she says.

Then she unfolds the sheet of paper.

It's Vero's precise enunciation of the word 'Sampan' that seems to have stopped my heart, so that I read the first paragraph on the page without breathing, with a ringing in my ears. Then I notice Vero's finger creeping carefully down the lines of type, and pausing from time to time, so I follow the finger, which has a nicely trimmed nail with magenta nail varnish on it, a colour said to denote common sense and a balanced outlook on life.

When I glance up over the tops of my glasses, the lawyer

Sue's head is an elegant blur.

Unlike my sister's methodical finger, my thoughts have stalled at the codicil's key item. I can't make them move.

At the same time, I'm not surprised by what I read, because the information fits into a pattern whose whole effect, like so much of Martin Klepka's effort, seemed intended to sabotage the rigorous order and symmetry of the things he made, including the austerely proportioned house we all lived in, which, however, could never discipline the limits of his world or the unruly shapes he twisted it into.

I'm also not surprised because ever since I was a kid, my father's least favoured, the one he cajoled into jumping from the piano, the one whose graduation he refused to attend, I've always gone on expecting something like this, the predictable and even banal warping factors in the narrative of my father's performances, like the ones he made a show of enjoying while mowing memories of the ghosts he'd brought with him from the Berlin Bauhaus after 1933 on to the impeccable nap of the lawn at the back of the house which will now move away from his history—from both that history's implacable order and from his attempts to escape from it.

Vero and I read the document shoulder to shoulder, having both had to hunt for our glasses, while the young lawyer Sue looks away from us across the room.

How did Vero guess?

The other child that our father had, our half-brother, whom we were never told about, has always been taken care of through a provision Agnes made after her husband died, when the Trust was set up. The child is intellectually disabled and needs care, and funds were set aside for that purpose by Agnes, separate from the Trust investment and undisclosed within it. When the house is sold, a proportional amount of the proceeds will go to support this child, if he is still alive. If he's died, the remaining funds allocated to his care will have been kept in escrow. The contact details of those charged with his care are appended.

The mother isn't identified in the document.

'You're right,' I say. 'The cleaner's kid.'

Vero takes her glasses off and closes her eyes.

'It's got to be.' Though I'm not surprised, you could say because this revelation fits the narrative probability of my father's life, which of course didn't end when he died, still my face has gone cold and I want to pant as if I've just finished my twenty lengths. The name Vero's already reminded me of is Sampan. 'Sampan,' I say. 'Sam-bloody-pan.'

'Good on her,' says Vero, opening her eyes. 'Agnes, I mean. Good on her. All those years. Dear wee thing.'

The 'dear wee thing' is Agnes, again, our mother, not the cleaner, or the child, but the calculation that spools haltingly through my brain puts the current age of my father's other child at about fifty-something, if indeed he's the Sam part of Sampan.

Out in the street, in the tumult of cars competing for innercity parking spaces, and the bustle of the back-to-work after lunch rush, with many different kinds of music coming in gusts of sound from the opening and closing doors of bars and restaurants, and with buses arriving and leaving in quick succession with hissing air-brakes, it's as though time has suddenly begun to speed up and disintegrate, and the narratives and meanings that depend on time passing smoothly have also begun to fall apart into randomness and incoherence. The city that had earlier in the day seemed so banal and grungy and dourly purposeful all at once seems full of untidy life, restless and impatient, breaking step, talking languages whose tones seem constantly to be inflected towards doubt and laughter.

We turn without consulting each other into a bar underneath Downstage Theatre, and order a glass of wine each.

'Well,' says Vero.

She doesn't at once pick up her glass. Where earlier in the lawyer's offices a familiar pugnacity had begun to harden her expression, now Vero looks calm.

'Well, well,' I say, as if to get our old game going again. 'Gosh.'

But Vero doesn't want to play. 'We all knew, really, didn't we,' she says. 'Except Mick. I mean, he *knew*, I reckon, but he didn't know he knew. Or he repressed the knowledge.' Her calm expression has been replaced by something like my father's stare. 'Don't look at me like that, Mr Smartypants.'

'Like what?' I say. 'I wasn't.'

'Of course the alternative,' says Vero, still not touching her wine, 'is that he stayed there in the house to keep an eye on the kid.'

'How likely is that? Even if we knew he lives round here. Or lives at all.' Unnecessarily, I add, 'I mean the kid.' Then I add, 'The middle-aged disabled man.' I'm getting drunk.

'Or to keep him out of the house,' Vero says, as if she's not talking to me but to some kind of Mick-intermediary.

'The middle-aged disabled man called Something Klepka,' I say, trying to get her off the subject of Mick. 'Our brother.'

'Or both,' says Vero. Now her eyes are focused on a plane somewhere between us.

'Come off it,' I say. 'You're starting to make stuff up in your head.' I give the table a professorial tap to regain her attention. 'And no, I didn't guess.'

Her eyes get my focal length and she does, finally, take a sip of the wine in front of her. 'Bull-*shit*,' she says, with that small-town emphasis on the 'shit'. 'Of course you bloody knew.' But then she pushes the glass away. 'Why didn't you stop me?'

'Stop you what?'

'Having another drink.'

'I didn't have to, did I.'

My sister heaves a big sigh. 'There's a time and place for everything,' she says, and isn't being ironic. And then she says, after reaching across the table for my hand, 'More to the point, are we going to meet this kid? And why don't you drink that for me? Pity to waste good wine.'

'Pretty much what Martin thought, obviously,' I say.

It's there between us, the shadow question that's cast by my bad-taste joke: *And what did Agnes think?* The answer should perhaps be in the minimal, unambiguous language of her codicil, whose words are not hers really, only their effect is. It would seem she didn't want us to know about the child or about how she felt. Though telling us she didn't want us to know about either of these things doesn't really tell us how she felt. And even then, she didn't really tell us 'in as many words' that she didn't want us to know, she just implied it. Or got her lawyers to imply it by sealing the implication in an envelope. Or the answer could be in the way she lived on in the house after her husband died and she'd carefully wound the business up, and sold the redundant real-estate including the warehouse and the workshops, and the back catalogue, and the current stock, and the design templates, and the marketing archive—all of which had been her domain—and even the good will, which was Martin Klepka's, and which she put a high price on, because the genius's clients were good, sustainable trade business.

'Where did you go?' asks Vero, giving me a poke.

'Agnes really sorted it all out, didn't she,' I say, beginning to answer the question I know we'll have to ask before long. I shouldn't be drinking Vero's glass of wine, but I already have. When I go to stand up, she gets one hand under my arm to steady me.

'One of us has to do it,' she says, and I think she means get pissed, not meet the love-child, if that's what he was. Is.

'Taxi?' she says.

There are some parked at the curb. But I march her with her hand still under my arm towards the pedestrian crossing that will turn us to face back the way we've come.

This already feels like an ending of some kind, but of course it's not. Professor Klepka, who isn't sad at the moment, and his sister who isn't bad, walk with studied sobriety back towards the house where all this began, and where it will probably end, whatever that means. I'm surprised by the steadiness not to say resoluteness of my sister's tread, one foot in front of the other, her hand under my arm occasionally giving a small directional hint.

We pass the bar where I know Micky used to spend time and where we sometimes met. A pleasant babble of conversation comes out into the street along with a woman taking a cigarette from her pack. It's mid-afternoon, but the bar on the corner with the betting monitors on the wall is about two-thirds full. I'll bet he kept going there, not as an extravagance of any kind, and not even as a regular relaxation, but because the place was one of his minimal necessities, part of the minimal, obsessive structure of his life, which wasn't any more 'empty' than the house he'd emptied of everything except what he needed.

Which raises another question. If he was using drugs again, where was he doing it? If they'd been in the house, the cops would have noticed and reported it. If an overdose killed Mick, they'd have seen signs of it. But he was just sitting in his La-Z-Boy, with the TV turned off, as if his quiet evening at home was over. The autopsy is sometime today and if there's meth in his system it will still show up, but it wasn't one of the bare essentials he kept in the house, any more than a hot-water jug was.

We're crossing the road at the Pirie Street junction, and Vero is ever so subtly keeping the pace on, and a hand under my arm, as if she wants to hurry but is being solicitous of me. A young woman jogs past us on the pedestrian crossing; she's got a toddler in a racy-looking pushchair.

'We used to call them strollers,' I say. 'That seems to have gone out of fashion.' The young woman's wearing tights and has a truly gorgeous arse, so gorgeous I almost let out an inappropriate sound of some kind, and I start to say, 'Jesus Christ, I loved being young,' but instead I keep answering questions I haven't asked yet. This time it's, 'What do you think Mick died of?'—only I say, 'Watching a blank TV screen never killed anybody, that I know of, anyway.'

The beautiful jogger's metronomic ponytail is conducting a little song of lust in my bloodstream as she goes swiftly up the hill and joins a small crowd of parents assembled outside the primary school, *Ach, die erste Liebe/ macht das Herz mächtig schwach*, but I don't stop and sing it, or hum it while we're walking, though I'd like to stop for a while.

'You okay, Sandy?' asks Vero.

I lean for a moment against the wall of Clyde Quay School. It is covered with a charming, colourful mural by the kids, in which people have smiles like curved orange segments, the sun as well, and there are profuse flowers all growing up straight out of bright green grass. We had a lot of fun when we were kids, we did different stuff from the others; sometimes it wasn't so much fun, it's true, but overall . . .

'It's okay, no rush,' says my sister, who's got what's sometimes called a 'thoughtful' side to her nature, which doesn't mean she thinks a lot, though perhaps she does, it means she cares about people, always did, even her dickhead husband. I'd quite like to sit down with my back to the mural, but instead I just close my eyes. A frantic jostle of pale and dark blotches is dancing beneath my eyelids. There's a technical name for the condition, but as yet I've no desire to know what that is. There's the racket of school breaking up for the day, kids yelling, the sounds of running feet. It's nice to listen without looking, and to let the world sway a little.

'What do you think Mick died of?' I ask Vero, just to keep it simple. I think that if she has a good enough answer I'll take it in, like a lungful of fresh air, and we'll get moving again.

I don't open my eyes when she puts her arms around me, and so for a moment it's possible to imagine that her springy hair is my mother's—they're about the same height—though her big pillowy breasts pushed against me at the bottom of my ribcage aren't my mother's. Agnes used to come and meet us from school. We boys wore sandals and shorts, and the girls wore cotton dresses and mostly had white ankle socks. There used to be a class picture in the house of Mick in 1958, when he was eight years old. Because he was tall for his age he was in the back row, at the end on the left, the top button of his shirt done up the way he preferred it, the only one in the class who did, and he and the kid next to him are leaning away from each other as if there's a wasp between them. Marty used to call it the fart photo.

'I think his time was up,' Vero says. 'I think he just ran out of it.'

'Don't you want to know why?'

'I don't think it makes any difference,' she says. 'Come on, man, we can't be seen doing brother–sister love outside a primary school, especially with you half-cut.'

I think Mick had been put on the end of a row in the class photo because that's where he belonged, at the edge. He was leaning away from the other kid because that kid wasn't part of his life, not because there was a wasp or a fart between them, and the other kid was leaning away from Michael Klepka because he was scared of him, most kids were. Mick wasn't violent, he just had limits. There were always non-negotiable limits to him that he wasn't going to go past—for example, taking swimming lessons, or later on turning the volume of his music down—and maybe his time was like that. There was an edge to it, pure and simple, and he got there and maybe even got his way.

We're heading up the hill to the house. A few shafts of sunlight are shooting intermittently through the clouds that are heaving along from north to south, and a flickering afternoon lightshow plays on the faded red wall of Martin Klepka's attempt to do what Farkas Molnár never could, actually build the fucking thing—*ein Einfamilienhaus. Einfamilien-haus!*

I drink a glass of water from the tap at the kitchen sink, and then go to the downstairs bathroom. It occurs to me as I cross the room from the sink to the bathroom that the glass I drank from is probably the one that last touched my brother's lips, before someone washed it. The other thing that Molnár probably didn't think of in 1922 was bathrooms, but my father put three of them into the house *he* built. So there! The one downstairs had a shower and a toilet, and a mirror wall above the washbasin, bog-standard now, so to speak, but verging on weird when we were kids. Upstairs there was an ensuite with the master bedroom, which had a large bath as well as a shower and a toilet, and the obligatory full-length mirror; and there was another with just a shower and a *separate* toilet, for the kids. Our friends from Clyde Quay were amazed. These provisions have also been described by architectural historians as 'innovative' for their time, but there had been a time in my father's life when amenities like them were unavailable—for example, while he was classed as a 'hostile alien' when he got to New Zealand in 1939. He had limits, too, like his favourite, Mick, but he preferred to make something of them, a statement rather than a subtraction.

In what I take to be 'Mick's bathroom' now that his entire inhabitation seems to have been limited to the downstairs floor of the house, there's almost nothing that tells me where the limits of his time were. He had one toothbrush and one partly used tube of toothpaste. He had one cake of nondescript supermarket soap that I have to retrieve from the shower, where I see his plastic container of a budget-brand shampoo. There's one damp towel folded neatly over the towel-rail, but it smells only of soap and dampness, not of my brother. There's the famous mirror wall, which, according to my father, was there because you needed to think of your body as a whole thing, not cut off at the waist or neck. He wasn't wrong about that.

'Want to have a look upstairs?' says Vero when I come back out. I sense that she's 'taking care', but, really, it's not called for. Mick's downstairs bathroom, like my memory of him leaning away from everyone else's time and place in his class photo of 1958, seems to have answered my question, the one I couldn't work out how or why to ask. Mick died because, finally, he'd leaned out of the frame.

But I don't try to find a way to say this to Vero, whose sturdy determination goes ahead of me up our father's famous stairs which, if we're to believe the architectural historians, were intended to, and did, or didn't, depending on the position you took up, resolve a problem bequeathed him by Molnár, namely, how to reconcile the geometrical section of a comfortable foot-lift at weary end of day with the demand of a rigorously stacked double cube whose uncomfortable proportions were glaringly revealed in the sketch that is now on display in the Bauhaus Archiv I visited in the company of Gertrud Schoening about seven years ago, when the conception of my or anyone's time running out didn't get any further than my maudlin, self-pitying statement 'I'm getting old', and her reasonable derision.

Martin Klepka's solution to the staircase involved leaning away from the problem. The stair-lifts got progressively lower as you approached the top. It got easier the higher you went. But, perversely, the time it took to get there increased as you got closer. 'Perverse' was one of the architectural critic's words he was proudest of, but for me it used to be maddening to feel my knees lifting a tiny bit less the closer I got to the top of the stairs. It seemed to be a vindictive thing to have thought of building into the *Einfamilienhaus*, the *Ein-familien-haus*, though perhaps, it now occurs to me, as Vero and I find it easier and easier but also slower and slower to get to the top floor, it also made tantalising our father's ascent to the room where he took his nap, sometimes, it would seem, with the mother of our half-brother, the dark-haired girl who used to clean the house on Fridays, when Agnes was at the textile studio, and we were all still at school, or so Martin Klepka thought.

Except that once his favourite was wagging school, and Mick later told us how he'd listened to the man he called Marty and the girl 'jumping on the bed' in the big room. But that didn't surprise us. He did that kind of thing all the time.

'Micky knew,' I say as we take the final, infuriating, shallow steps up to the top floor of the house. 'He knew more about it than any of us.'

Vero doesn't turn around, and nothing in her deportment tells me she's taking any notice of what I'm saying, but when we get into what used to be her room, she does turn, and I see before me the sister who's had the nous to get a life, keep fit, hang on to her capital, and along the way exert some willpower over her drinking problem. If there's emotional business to transact at this point she's not interested—as she'd said not long ago, 'There's a time and place for everything.'

'Gutted,' she says, meaning the house, not herself, though she may be for all I can see.

Then my phone buzzes, and she gives a jump, as if her nerves are after all barely under control. It's a rote text from the hospital: please make an urgent appointment re autopsy and remember to nominate a funeral director. There's a number to call back.

I give the phone to Vero because I can see that she's in control mode, and I go along the corridor to the room that used to be mine, then to Mick's, which was next to mine, which meant that mine was therefore closest to his music, and then down the passage to Martin and Agnes's room, the largest, three-quarters of the house's top cube, with windows on three sides. All the rooms are empty, of furniture but also of any other kind of presence, which is to say of time, as if Mick had performed some kind of historical purge as he emptied the house. Agnes got rid of the original drapes years ago, not long after her husband's heart attack, but the furnishings that were left were all top-of-the-line showpieces of the Klepka enterprise, and they were all still intact when she died. Back then, twenty-six years ago, I stayed for the last time in my old room whose Klepka textile curtains had been replaced by Klepka wooden blinds. The rooms were musty as if they hadn't been aired or cleaned for a long time, which they probably hadn't, apart from the one Agnes had continued to sleep in, the big one, which got the northern sun from the east when it rose above Mount Victoria, all the way around to the west when it went down behind Brooklyn.

The sun is heading towards that western ridge now, and the empty room feels naked as the bright, late sun shooting out of clouds comes in through the three big square windows facing that way, their joined-together lateral proportions of course exactly Fibonacci-commensurate with the dimension of their wall. But this familiar order, the nearest thing to a haunting in the house, or the nearest thing to a history, is no defence against the room's utter emptiness, its nakedness.

A woman's voice calls from downstairs—'Hello? Anybody home?'

I step into the passage at the same time as Vero. She still has my cellphone to her ear, so I call out that yes, there's somebody *home*, and we hurry down the famous Klepka stairs, which get thicker and faster as we approach the bottom, with the word 'home' suspended somewhere behind us in the big empty room.

It's a young Asian woman—she's standing just inside the door to the room Mick had subtracted his home into. She's dressed somewhat formally, in a neat skirt and jacket suit, with a pair of nice black pumps on, and her hair in a bun.

My first thought is that she's a real-estate agent, and much too quick off the mark, but as soon as she speaks I know she's the woman who found Mick dead in front of his TV yesterday.

'I'm sorry,' she says, 'the door was open?' Her questioning inflection implies a kind of permission-granted, as if she might have come through the open door at other times.

'Okay,' says Vero into my phone, while looking at the young woman, 'the Wilson Funeral Home, Adelaide Road. And we'll see you tomorrow morning.' Still looking at the woman, she says to me, 'That was the funeral home. And the autopsy stuff tomorrow morning, at the hospital again. How do you turn this off?' She gives me the phone without taking her eyes off the woman, who has one hand against the door frame, as if her entry is only provisional after all. Then Vero takes a step towards her, and begins to hold out her hand, but then holds out both arms.

'Hello,' she says. 'You must be Mick's friend. I'm his sister, Veronica.'

I've got the phone to my ear and am listening to its disconnected hum, then realise what I'm doing and turn it off. The two women are embracing awkwardly, as if neither of them has expected to, and I feel I should do the same, but the young woman steps aside into the room and takes up a position next to Mick's bed, where his coat is folded neatly on top of the faded Klepka bedspread.

'I brought his coat back,' she says, gesturing at it with an open palm, as if she's rehearsed this moment. 'I didn't touch anything.'

'What's your name, dear?' says Vero.

'May,' says the young woman, and stops there. She's in

her twenties, I'd guess.

'Well, May,' says Vero, 'thank you for taking care of Mick. I mean, tidying up and everything.'

'I just called the police,' says May. 'I didn't touch anything.'

'I'm sure you didn't, dear,' says Vero, giving me a look. 'This is Mick's older brother, Alastair.'

The young woman's hand when I shake it is expressionless—it doesn't grip mine, but just rests there until I let it go. Obviously, the passivity of her hand is how this transaction is going to be conducted from her side. What am I supposed to do: ask her what kind of friend she was? Did she have an understanding with Mick that she could come into the house any time she wanted?

But then she seems to answer my questions, as if she's anticipated them and rehearsed what to say. 'I've never been in Mick's house before,' she says. 'I mean, before yesterday. The door wasn't locked.' Then she adds, in a phrase that seems borrowed or learned from American television dialogue, 'I'm very sorry for your loss.'

'But he left his coat at your place?' I've heard what the police had to say about this. 'And his wallet?'

'Yes,' says May. She seems to be both asserting something and not giving anything away—standing firmly just behind her passivity.

'I'm sorry, May,' says Vero, as if to cut me off. 'I'd offer you a cup of tea, but there's really nothing in the house at all. Except beer,' she adds.

'No thank you,' says May, still seeming to wait.

'Why was that?' I say.

The look she gives me is certainly direct enough, even

if it's opaque. 'Why was what?' she says.

'Why did he leave his coat at your place?' I was a little bit drunk before, but the irritation I'm feeling now isn't because of that, it's because the house seems to be vaporising all the information that comes into it, and I want something, anything really, that will fix what's going on in a time and place where I can get my head around it, and make sense of it, and stop this meandering around after ghosts.

'Does it really matter, Sandy?' says Vero, trying to cut me off again.

'Mick was in a hurry to get home,' says May, and now there are two spots of colour in her carefully made-up cheeks.

'Was he?' I say. 'Why was that? Why was my brother in a hurry?'

Vero's hand squeezes my arm at the same time as the young woman May makes a hissing sound and lifts Mick's coat from the bed. She reaches inside it and takes out an old wallet, which she opens and throws on the bed.

'See for yourself,' she says. 'I didn't touch anything.' Then she turns and walks out with loud clicks of her heels on the wooden floor.

Vero gives my arm a vicious pinch and calls out 'May!' but the front door slams. 'You're a miserable prick, you know that?' says my suddenly furious sister. 'A pompous, judgemental, overbearing arsehole. What did you have to do that for?'

I don't want to sit in the La-Z-Boy and there's nowhere else except Mick's neatly made-up bed, so I sit on the edge of it and pick up his old leather wallet. It's the nearest thing to a meaningful object so far in the whole fucking day, even allowing for the codicil with its not-quite-there trace of Agnes, and the wallet even has a history of sorts—the man he called Marty gave it to him when he left high school, along with a wristwatch and a packet of condoms.

'What did Martin give you when you left school?' I ask my sister. He gave me a course of driving lessons, which I completed, successfully. Mick refused to learn to drive unless 'Marty' taught him.

Inside his wallet, what might be thought of in Geertzian terms as the 'thick description' of the event we're trying but failing to understand suddenly gets thin. There's not a lot we can 'include in the consultable record'. There's no way to go from 'inscription' to 'specification'. There isn't any sense. There's no conclusion to come to. There's a public library card, two twenty-dollar notes, a little bit of change in a zip-up pocket, and a betting slip from the TAB. The utter poverty of meaning is unbearable.

The bed sinks a little as Vero sits down beside me. She's breathing heavily, and I know she's turned herself sideways to look at me, because I can feel her breath on my neck.

'Agnes took me out for lunch at the Monde Marie and gave me some nice lingerie,' says Vero. 'She also told me not to let boys cajole me into fucking them, not that she put it like that.' Her breath continues to puff against my neck. 'Don't be so angry, Sandy. It wasn't the poor girl's fault, whatever happened. She got herself all dressed up. Why not assume she cared about Mick?'

'She was a hooker,' I say, not looking at my sister but at the carefully edited mise-en-scène of the La-Z-Boy and the TV set, with the concreted backyard beyond through the French doors. A wash of late-afternoon light is refracted across the beautifully ordered stripes of the tongue-and-groove matai floorboards, which 'Marty' used to love oiling with his own concoction of linseed, turpentine and beeswax, and then getting us to skate around the floor with socks on, to cut back to the shine.

'Of course she was,' says Vero. 'With your superior powers of discernment you'd have grasped that instantly.'

When I do turn away from the still-life arrangement on the floor of the big living room of the house, with its odd diagonals of amber afternoon light, and face my sister again, she's looking where I was a second ago, across the room and out at the yard.

'I feel sorry for the poor buggers who'll have to rip that lot up,' she says, as if in her mind the house has already been sold to some connoisseurs bent on restoring it. 'Sooner them than me.' Then she gets to her feet. 'Sooner them than me,' she says again. 'Bloody Mick. It was never going to be easy getting rid of him.' She pulls the French doors shut and shoots the brass bolts that Martin Klepka chose with such care.

'What do you want to do now?' I ask, needing more than anything to fall back on Mick's bed and go to sleep.

'I'm going to tell Mick's friends,' says Vero. 'I'm not stopping here a moment longer. It's starting to give me the creeps.' She extends the handle of her trundle suitcase with a smart snap. 'Come on, Sandy,' she says. 'I'm not doing this on my own.'

The bar is nice and warm after the blustery chill of the walk along Cambridge Terrace, and I take a seat at one of the few remaining vacant tables while Vero talks to the barman. I watch my sister taking care. She leans over the bar, talking quietly to the guy, whose patient smile suddenly shuts down as he takes Vero's hand in both of his. Then he's pointing up at a shelf of whiskies, wagging his finger in their direction. Vero's nodding and pointing too. The guy reaches up and takes down a bottle of Jameson's. I know the label because it was Mick's favourite, we used to have one or two when our trustees' meetings were held in this bar back then.

Veronica holds the bottle of Jameson's aloft and is noticed.

'Anybody here a friend of Micky Klepka's?' she shouts.

A whole lot of heads crane and swivel and give Micky's sister their close attention, like punters watching the leaders in the home straight, the way I remember they did on the occasions when Jilly dragooned me into the members' stand at Ellerslie. Their expressions are pretty uniformly thrilled at first, as if they've finally seen a winner, but then they get it.